RESCUING REGINA

LEE SAVINO

FREE BOOK

Get your FREE copy of Beauty & The Lumberjacks: https://BookHip.com/WZLTMQX

After this logging season, I'm never having sex again. Because: *reasons*.

But first, I have a gig earning room and board and ten thousand dollars by 'entertaining' eight lumberjacks.

Eight strong and strapping Paul Bunyan types, big enough to break me in two.

There's Lincoln, the leader, the stern, silent type...

Jagger, the Kurt Cobain look-alike, with a soul full of music and rockstar moves...

Elon & Oren, ginger twins who share everything...

Saint, the quiet genius with a monster in his pants...

Roy and Tommy, who just want to watch...

And Mason, who hates me and won't say why, but on his night tries to break me with pleasure...

They own me: body, mind and orgasms.

But when they discover my secret—the reason I'm hiding from the world—everything changes.

Click here to read Beauty and the Lumberjacks for free

RESCUING REGINA

A woman on the wrong side of the law. The sheriff who demands her submission.

Regina doesn't want to steal, but after losing her job, she has no other way to pay the bills. Her crime spree ends when she's caught by Cole Townsend, the local sheriff. He's hot, he's dominant, he's decided to claim her, and he won't tolerate anything but her perfect obedience.

After taking her over his knee, Cole gives Regina an ultimatum: Submit to him or go to jail.

1

The car rolled to a stop, and I peered through the rain-studded windshield. A high chain link fence rose between us and the warehouse parking lot.

"There it is," I said. The headlights pooled on the pavement, illuminating our prize.

"Jackpot," said my greasy-haired companion. "Just where you'd said it'd be."

"Of course," I snorted. I was a little drunk. "I only worked here since I was sixteen."

"How do we get it out? Climb the fence?"

"No need. The lock is just for show. It doesn't work."

"You'd think he'd lock it up tighter."

"Mr. Roberts is a trusting guy." I felt a pang, remembering when I'd been one of the people he could trust. "Come on."

"Wait." My companion—Benji? Barry? I couldn't remember his name—picked up his blunt. He took a pull before offering it to me.

Wrinkling my nose, I took it and mimicked him, pulling the sweet smoke into my lungs. The whiskey was wearing off, and a little marijuana would take the edge off my self-disgust. If I was lucky, it would keep me from wondering why I was drunk and getting high. Why I was with a loser about to rob my former employer. It was a night of firsts.

"Here goes nothing," I muttered, and exited the car. The first foil came when I saw the shiny new lock and chain on the gate. That hadn't been there a few hours ago.

"What's wrong?" My partner in crime still hadn't left the car.

"It's locked," I called back. "I'm going to climb the fence, see if there are bolt cutters or something."

I faced the fence with more confidence than I felt. As I hooked my fingers into the links and prepared to hoist myself up, the heavens opened. Rain poured down as if to say, *this is a bad idea.*

Two feet off the ground, my legs weakened. I shouldn't have had that last shot.

"Oi," I called to the pothead behind the wheel. "A little help here?"

A police siren came alive behind me. The shock nearly gave me a heart attack. I fell from the fence and sprawled on the ground. Blue and red light washed over me with the rain.

My partner in crime put his car in reverse and hit the gas. The getaway vehicle's doors flapped open as it squealed past the cop car.

"Hey, wait!" I got to my feet, only to squint into flashing lights as the sheriff's vehicle rolled closer, cutting off my escape.

I could only stand there, squinting into the headlights. It probably was Officer Smith or Officer Johnson. Both knew me from my mildly delinquent days as a frustrated teen who sometimes cut school. I could already imagine their smirks.

"What are you doing here, Regina?" came a deep voice.

Oh no. No, no, no.

Instead of porky Smith or flatulent Johnson, Sheriff Townsend unfolded from his vehicle.

I'd known him as a kid and he'd always been serious, stern, and an absolute stickler for rules. Age hadn't softened him. Not that he was old—twenty-eight, only six years older than me. Not that old at all.

He'd entered the academy at eighteen and worked his way up through the force, and though some say he won the sheriff election by luck, most would agree he deserved the office. He was hardworking, humble, even as he radiated quiet power.

Oh, and he was hot. The hottest man for three counties, maybe more. In high school, I heard of girls who'd speed just so he'd pull them over. He'd call the girl's parents, and they'd invite him over for dinner.

He'd always had a gentle and firm authority that made the most protective fathers offer their daughter's hand in marriage. He was perfect.

Damn him.

Cole's long legs carried him a few feet away from me. The light outlined a fine, strapping chest and arms that could probably bench press Smith and Johnson. He had a waistline that had never met a donut in its life.

"Sheriff." I wished I didn't have mud and pine needles all over my jeans. "Lovely evening for a stroll."

"You're trespassing, Regina. This whole road is private property." I heard the frown in his voice.

"I work here."

"Not anymore. Mr. Roberts gave you notice today."

My mouth fell open. I knew small town gossip was fast, but not that fast. "How do you know?"

"Mr. Roberts told me."

"Well…" I crossed my arms in front of my chest. I couldn't quite pull it off, because my boobs got in the way. "Did he tell you that he didn't even give me a reason?"

"He doesn't have to. It's a right-to-work state."

"I've worked here since I was sixteen!" The rain came down harder and I gritted my teeth, realizing how ridiculous it was to have an argument with this man. He'd caught me in the act. If it'd been any other officer, I'd probably be face down in the mud, getting Mirandized.

"Get in the car."

"No." I really was out of my mind. My head tipped back as Cole Townsend advanced, all six feet of him. He'd always been tall, even as a kid. And serious. A nice guy but he didn't have to work hard to look dangerous. Nobody messed with Sheriff Townsend.

Except me.

He held the flashlight up so I couldn't see him, but he didn't shine it in my eyes. The shadow silhouetted the clean line of his jaw. I couldn't see his face, but I knew he had serious green eyes, and blond hair he'd worn in a buzz cut since joining the force.

He was just delicious.

"I forgot my wallet when I left. It must have fallen out of my purse, and I'd never drive without a license. That's why what's-his-name gave me a ride. Now, if you'll excuse me…" I turned back to the fence and started to climb it. Well, tried anyway. My limbs wouldn't work right. I ended up pulling on the links, grunting in frustration.

Heat hit my back and I froze.

"Nice try," Cole literally breathed down my neck. His arm wrapped around me to slide my wallet out of the front of my jeans' pocket.

"Why, Sheriff Townsend," I cooed, trying to keep my cool even though my panties were swimming. "Is that a gun or are you excited to see me?"

"It's a gun." He pulled me to face him, away from the fence. "How much did you have to drink?"

I held up two fingers and giggled.

"I don't believe you. One shot wouldn't do this to you."

I held up five fingers.

He shook his head in disapproval.

"Oh come on, Sheriff. You never got drunk and went a little wild?"

"No." He pulled me towards the car. I went willingly, until I remembered my plan to be a pain in the ass.

"You really are Mr. Perfect."

"I am not."

"Really?" I tugged my hand out of his. "Tell me one thing you've done that would get you in trouble if anyone knew."

"I'm about to do something right now."

My eyebrows shot up at his dark tone. I was almost afraid to ask.

Almost. "Like what?"

But Mr. Perfect wasn't in the mood to talk. He bent, tossed me over his shoulder, and strode the rest of the way to the car with me protesting. His arm clamped over the back of my thighs. I felt higher than I had after smoking the pot. Upside down, I got an eyeful of his taut sheriff buns.

He set me down and opened the car door. "Get in."

I stood my ground.

"Regina, I'm not going to ask you again."

A few raindrops spattered. "Fine," I said. "But only because I need a ride."

He did a sweep of the area before getting back in the car and slowly pulling down the dark, private road.

Despite everything that had happened, I felt giddy. I was in a car with Cole Townsend! I bounced on the seat, trying not to giggle like a moron.

"You want to tell me why you were trespassing on your former employer's land?"

"No."

"Regina."

"Why do you call me that? Everyone else calls me Gina."

"Regina is your full name. I prefer it."

"I do too. It means 'queen.' Yours means 'black rock that comes out of the ground.'" I pressed my face to the bars between him and me. The speedometer read fifteen miles per hour. We were on a private road and he was still following the speed limit. "Can we go faster? I wanna hear the siren."

"No."

"You're no fun."

"I don't think you're taking this as seriously as you should be."

"Why didn't you just say you wanted to get me alone?" I blew on the back of his neck and watched in fascination as his body went rigid. "You can handcuff me anytime you like. I bet all the girls say that to you."

"Quiet."

I wasn't totally unattractive, but I was out of this guy's league. I'd never dare act this way if I wasn't so tipsy. "I'll get you off, if you get me off," I purred. "If you know what I mean—"

The car lurched to a stop and Cole got out. I shut up, suddenly nervous. I squeaked in surprise when he threw my door open and dragged me outside.

The night seemed darker, colder as he loomed over me.

"Let me get this straight," he said through gritted teeth. "You're offering sexual favors so I'll go easy on you?"

I gulped but I wasn't in a position to deny it. Cole hadn't charged me with a crime yet, but if I could get out of trouble by getting on my knees, I had to do it.

"Answer me." His voice sounded harsher in the darkness.

"Yes."

His grabbed my hips and drew me closer. Without another word, he undid the top button of my jeans.

My gut lurched. "Please," I said, because I'd imagined this moment with Cole Townsend many, many times, but never like this. This felt wrong.

He stopped.

I thought of what would happen to my mom if I went to jail, and shook my head. "Never...never mind."

"Turn around and put your hands on the trunk of the car."

I obeyed, feeling a little sick. He ran his hands over my back before tugging down my jeans. Immediately my pussy creamed. I was hot for him.

It still felt cheap.

Cole pushed me lower, so I almost kissed the trunk of the car. With my backside pointed at him, I spread my legs as far as I could with my jeans still on. I waited in silent acquiescence, telling myself at least it was Cole, and not some other dickhead officer.

The rain kept falling. I stared at the water droplets on the trunk of the car.

Smack! Something hit my panty-clad bottom, hard enough to drive me forward. My body jerked in shock.

Cole followed it up with a pattern of strikes to my ass while I bent over, too stunned to call out. Then his palm caught the underside of my bottom. The sting penetrated through the haze of booze and weed, and I gasped and reared up, trying to escape.

He put his hand on the back of my neck, holding me down as he did it again.

"Cole! That hurts."

"Good." A flurry of swats had me squirming. I burned with more than just the pain from the flat of his hand, though. I was a grown woman of twenty-two, bent over the back of a cop car getting her bottom spanked like a naughty little girl.

My insides tingled.

He stopped long enough to peel down my panties. I caught my breath, waiting for him to take me for real. But no, his hand came down again, a flurry of spanks that made me cry out. Each smack felt harder than the last. I tried wriggling, but he gripped the back of my neck harder, holding me still. Not being able to move somehow added to the pain. My buns were going to be red hot by the end of this, and I couldn't escape.

If this was a new take on corporal punishment, I didn't like it. I'd rather just go to jail.

He continued spanking me, adding a lecture in a low, hard voice.

"You are in huge trouble. You're going to do as I say and keep your mouth shut. And you don't ever, ever proposition a man of the law. Ever, ever again." His hand came down particularly hard at that point.

"Okay, okay," I shouted.

"I mean it, Regina. You find yourself in the back of a cop car again, you keep a polite tone and you don't disrespect the officer, or yourself, by offering sexual favors. Do you promise?"

"I promise!" Goddammit. I was wet and cold and my butt stung so bad. His hands were made of concrete. "Just stop. You're hurting me!"

"I would never, ever hurt you."

I whimpered as the flat of his hand hit one cheek and pain reverberated through my already sore bottom. "What do you call this then?"

"A wake up call."

Sheriff Sadist smacked me on the other butt cheek. The force of his palm drove away any lingering numbness left by the pot or booze. He paused.

I held my breath, hoping it was over. When Cole touched me again, he stroked my bottom gently.

"Are you okay?" Did I hear a tinge of concern in his voice?

I nodded frantically, hoping he wouldn't touch me lower and find out just how okay I was. I felt tingly all over, and not just from the pain. The sting awakened something deeper. Not just arousal, though I felt that very faintly, a prickle between my legs. He could tell me to do anything and I would, without asking questions.

That scared me more than anything.

"Good." His voice hardened. "You do as I say, and you don't give me any lip." He emphasized by squeezing one hot butt cheek, and I went up on my tiptoes. "Understand?"

I sagged against the car, trying to catch my breath.

"The correct answer is *yes, sir*," he prompted.

"Yes, sir." I felt numb. Cole Townsend had spanked me. I still couldn't believe it.

My burning ass told me to believe it.

"Now we're going to get back in the car. We're going to settle this mess tonight, one way or another." He pulled up my panties and helped me up. How could hands that caused so much pain be so gentle?

I went to pull up my jeans, and he caught my arm.

"Leave them down." His voice cracked like a shot.

My face heated despite the cool night air. We were on a private road, surrounded by a pine forest, but the humiliation still stung. I tottered back to the car, jeans around my knees. My disciplinarian brought up the rear. He helped me into the car, and paused. I blinked up at him. I must have had a frightened look on my face, because he gently brushed my hair back.

"You're going to be okay," he said.

I shifted on the seat and whimpered.

"Let's get you home."

2

I spent the car ride squirming on my hot bottom, wondering what the heck had just happened. Once again, I'd gotten in trouble. Once again, Cole came to my rescue.

He'd spanked me, but I couldn't think about that. I couldn't get my pot-addled brain around it at all.

A part of me knew I deserved it.

Cole stayed silent, letting me stew in my thoughts as his car rolled through the night. I pressed my forehead against the cold glass and closed my eyes.

Ever since I came to our little town, I'd been trying to escape. My parents moved here for my dad's factory job, a job he would lose anyway when he started drinking again. I was six and the most jaded kid ever. For some reason, our new neighbor took it upon herself to drag me to Sunday School.

The lesson was on Noah's ark. One of the students, a little blonde girl my age, asked the teacher what the animals ate all those months on the boat.

"Probably bunnies," I said loudly. "They have lots of babies. Because they're always screwing."

The teacher blustered for a moment. "Cole," she called to an older boy, sitting up very straight, wearing a perfectly pressed suit. "Will you sit by Regina and help her get settled in? She just moved here."

The blond boy nodded, polite and stern even though he couldn't be more than twelve. He came and sat beside me, and I tried not to look too pleased. The little girl who had asked the question shot daggers at me with her eyes. I stuck my tongue out at her and cozied up to my handsome new babysitter.

"Hello, I'm Cole," he said. "Welcome to Licking Hole."

I sniggered. "Do you know what that means?"

"Yes." He fixed me with a level stare. "Do you?"

I took a moment to study him. At twelve, Cole was already a dreamboat. He was clean and serious, without a spot of dirt on him. I was wearing a little dress with no tights. The skirt had a tear in the corner and had dirt stains from when I'd shut it in the car door. I was gross and disheveled, and desperate to impress this older boy. When I had announced where I was moving, the big kids at the trailer park had told me exactly what the name of my town could mean. I didn't quite believe them, but if it would help me make an impression on this good-looking young man, I was willing to spill the beans.

"I do," I said. "I bet you don't."

"A licking hole is where hunters put salt to attract deer, so they can shoot them. That's what it means."

"No, it doesn't," I sneered. "It's when someone puts their tongue—"

"Regina?" The teacher cut in brightly, oblivious to my

and Cole's conversation. "Do you want to tell the class where you live?"

"No," I said, but caved after encouragement. "Shady Park."

"That's a trailer park," the girl with blonde curls giggled.

My cheeks went hot.

"That's right, Lucy," the teacher said, oblivious to the classism going on. Lucy waited until the teacher turned her back before sticking her tongue out at me.

I waited until we were in line to go up to the service before I yanked on her perfect curls.

Lucy howled.

I started to make my escape when someone pulled me back. Cole Townsend, tall and prim, had my arm in a lock.

"Let go," I said even though I liked the attention.

"I'm supposed to watch over you," he said, very sternly, and took my hand.

He held it all through the service, only letting go to hold the hymnal between us during songs. He pointed out the words. Afterward, he escorted me down to the fellowship hall again, got me lemonade and cookies, and took me to the bathroom. He waited for me outside the door until I was done, and checked to make sure I'd washed my hands.

By the end of the service, I was in love.

But then noon came, and the neighbor took me back to the trailer park. She never took me to church again. I tried walking there and got lost. Mom and Dad found me and I was grounded until school started. I got through summer dreaming of the blond boy in a suit, with more reserve and poise than a politician. I couldn't wait for school, only to learn that Cole was six years older than me. Lucy was my age, though. The little blonde witch was just waiting to pull my hair.

Even though we lived in a small town, I didn't see Cole a lot. We moved in different circles. Each time, my heart beat with excitement. And each time, the space between us widened into a chasm.

Now he was sheriff, and I was in the back of a cop car, where a kid from a trailer park belonged. My life was over. Other than my burning buns, I felt relief.

The car stopped and I opened my eyes, half expecting to see the little police station on Main Street. Despite its unfortunate name, Licking Hole was a quaint little town, with enough money to build a beautiful brick library, a white columned courthouse and sheriff's office.

I didn't expect to see a little brick rancher with a neat lawn. Cole had brought me home all right, but not to my mother's trailer. I'd only seen this place a few times but I knew exactly where I was.

Cole's house.

3

I sat up straight, stinging butt forgotten.

"What are you doing? Shouldn't we be at the station?"

"I wanted someplace quiet. We're going to have a chat."

The word "chat" had never been so ominous. My bottom still stung. I shifted uneasily, and he told me I could pull up my jeans.

Well, thank you very much. I bit back my response as he came around and opened my door.

What was going on? Why was I at his house? I couldn't even wrap my mind around the fact that he'd spanked me.

I hesitated long enough for him to order me out.

"Yes sir," I said with just enough mockery to keep my pride. But when I slid out of the seat my legs wobbled and I would've fallen if he didn't catch me.

"Easy." The mess of what I'd drunk and smoked that night was taking its toll, both abandoning me in my time of need and leaving me weak. My head felt foggy, and I needed food, stat.

Cole's hard muscled arm around my waist felt so good. I

let myself lean on him up to the door. He took his arm away to unlock the door, and I hated losing his warm support, even for a second. The thought startled me into bitchiness.

"What, locked? Are you afraid of big, bad criminals?"

"Not afraid. Just smart. I know the monsters are out there."

"And I don't?"

"You got into the car with one."

"Benny? He's harmless."

"I didn't mean Benny."

His dark tone made me swallow my comments for a moment.

Before I could say anything, he led me to a bench in the entryway and had me sit. To my surprise, he knelt and took off my shoes. His proximity made me flush, so to distract myself I studied his house. Sunken living room with couches and a TV. Carpet looked new. So did the hardwood floors. Everything was clean, if a little sparse.

"Nice place," I said.

"Thank you."

He'd bought this house while I was in college. Cole always so serious and ahead of his time. Lifeguard at fifteen. Police academy at eighteen. Elected sheriff before thirty.

The house was probably just part of the plan. A white picket fence, a wife and two point five kids were probably next on his to-do list.

I studied the gorgeous wood floors, feeling suddenly out of place.

"You still haven't told me why I'm here."

He stood, and kept his eyes on me as he took off his badge and his belt. The sight of his gun made me stifle a gasp.

"Let's get you cleaned up first." He turned on bare feet.

I didn't move. After a few steps, he realized I wasn't following. "Regina, come on."

"Is this where you take all your perps?"

"I'm off duty. You aren't a perp."

But I was. He didn't even know how much. "Then what am I doing here?"

He saw the worry in my face, because he sighed and motioned to the couch. "Sit." Even without his badge and in bare feet, he was still the picture of authority. Under different circumstances, I'd enjoy teasing the seriousness in his hazel eyes.

"Regina," he warned.

I gulped but held my ground. "I'd rather stand. Are you going to read me my rights?"

"Do you want me to?"

"What is this, Cole?"

"Sheriff Townsend."

"Whatever. I've known you all my life," I said.

"That's why you're here. Sit down, Regina." I did and regretted it when he towered over me, a stern teacher chastising a naughty schoolgirl. The sheriff and the town screw up. "You're in a load of trouble."

I nodded. I couldn't refute that.

"Getting drunk, leaving the bar with Benny-whose record isn't pretty, trespassing on private property—"

"Getting drunk isn't a crime." Neither was getting into a car with Benny from the bar, even if he did have a criminal record. I wondered why Cole included that in my list of sins.

At least he hadn't found out about the weed.

"Then there's this." He dangled the baggie of pot in front of my face. Benny must've flung it out of his car when he was gone. Or, more likely, it fell out in his haste to get away. Just my luck.

"That was Benny's."

He kept glaring at me. I squirmed.

"I just smoked a little for nerves. I've never done it before."

"Never?"

I hesitated.

"Stand up." His whip-like tone startled me to my feet. He turned me around and bent me over.

Oh, not again.

Cole swatted me through my jeans, hard.

"Ow." How he'd gotten it to hurt through the denim, I had no idea. Maybe my behind was bruised from my last beating.

"That's the consequence of lying. Sit down again."

"I don't wanna," I pouted, rubbing my butt. But I obeyed with a little wince. I'd started to learn disobedience wasn't the way to go. He'd more than proved he was willing to spank me.

"Now you're going to tell me the truth or you'll regret it. How much of this stuff did you have with you?"

"Just that." I didn't protest that it was Benny's again, guessing that Cole just wanted to know my involvement. He seemed pretty focused on me, and only me.

"This is your first time smoking pot?"

"Third or fourth," I said. "The last times were all in college."

A little of his anger ebbed away. "Were you planning to sell this?"

I started to answer then hesitated. He said no lying.

"I thought about selling it, yes," I said with total honesty. "I need money."

"If I find you've lied to me—"

"Cole, I swear I only thought about it. Benny mentioned

dealing it, I decided it wouldn't be right. The only reason I got in the car with him was because I was tipsy at the bar. Believe me, it won't ever happen again. And if this is some sort of sting, I'm happy to testify to Benny's statement about selling, if you want."

After my little outburst, Cole relaxed so much he looked like a different man. He sat down on the couch beside me, like I was a friend and not a suspect. Relief washed over me, so intense it made me wonder about the depth of my feelings for my sheriff. Maybe I hadn't gotten over my schoolgirl crush.

"This isn't a sting. We know Benny's getting pot with intent to deal. I was afraid you were caught up in it. You shouldn't be anywhere near Benny or the people he deals with."

"Well, no worries about that. The man is disgusting."

Cole nodded, looking pleased. I felt more confused than ever.

"What is this anyway? A new form of interrogation? Your own version of good cop/bad cop? Stern cop and...sadistic spanking cop?"

He almost smiled. Almost. Which was fine because I wasn't trying to be funny. "I did get carried away with the spanking."

"Yes, what was that? You freaked me out." I shifted on my seat, pressing my legs together. I'd been more than freaked out. I'd been scared and aroused. It was the arousal, mainly, that freaked me out.

His quick glance at my legs told me he hadn't missed the movement.

"You were belligerent, and I wanted to get your attention. I couldn't have you repeating that behavior again."

"Being a smart aleck?"

"Propositioning a cop."

"I didn't know that was such a serious crime."

"It is, because some men on the force would take you up on it. And I can't have that."

"If you don't trust your men, there's no need to take it out on me. I doubt you spank all the people who try to bribe cops."

"No. Only you."

I felt perversely happy knowing I was the only one.

"And it's not that my men are corrupt. They're good people, for the most part, but you would be more than a little temptation."

I blinked at that.

He seemed pleased with my surprise. Leaning into me, he brushed his arm against mine. "So you see, I had to nip that behavior in the bud." His tone gentled. "Did I scare you?"

"No, not really. Well, maybe at first. But a little bud nipping never hurt anyone."

His eyes crinkled, and my panties gave up hope of ever being dry again. I hadn't meant to be flirty, but now that he'd taken it that way, warmth rushed over me.

I licked my lips and he focused his gaze on my mouth. Arousal hit me so hard I felt dizzy.

Oh my god, were we having a moment?

I shivered and my nipples hardened.

"The truth is," he said, "I could charge you, but I'd rather handle things differently."

What were we talking about? Oh right, my crimes.

"I'm okay with that." I liked the idea of Cole handling me.

"You might not agree when you know what it entails.

When I say you're in serious trouble, I mean it, Regina. And not just because of the stunt you pulled tonight."

A part of me felt relief that he might know about all the ways I'd broken the law, even before I got fired. Nothing got past those hazel eyes. His lashes were long as a girl's, and dark brown, the color of chocolate. Yum.

Now I was hungry.

"Regina, focus. How much?"

"What?" I'd missed the question.

"How much money do you need?"

All the warmth sucked out of my body. I sat up, muscles stiffening. Cole put his hand on my knee, but the reassuring touch wasn't enough to calm me down.

"I don't know. A lot."

Admitting that I needed money was more humiliating than the spanking, than being manhandled by my lifelong crush, than being forced to totter to the car with my jeans around my thighs.

"Your mom's been sick for..."

"Awhile," I whispered.

He nodded. "Okay."

"Okay? Just okay? It's not okay, Cole." I tore my gaze from his dreamboat eyes. What was I doing in this house, sitting next to this perfect man? Any other girl would kill to take my place. Of course, they'd be here because he asked them out on a date, nice and proper, and invited them in afterwards for a nightcap. He'd put his hand on their knee and it would be just the beginning...

My stomach soured. I didn't deserve to be on the couch with this golden boy. "You should just charge me," I muttered.

"I'm not going to do that. There will be consequences, but instead of the law, you'll be answering to me."

The thought of answering to Sheriff Sadist and his iron hand made me shiver. And not because I was afraid. The tingles in my panties had only grown stronger, spreading through my entire body whenever he touched me. Even when he had been spanking me.

Especially when he spanked me. I had to get out before I lost my mind.

"Sheriff Cole bending the rules? That doesn't sound like you. You can't just go around bending the rules for just anyone." I risked a glance at his stunning profile. To my surprise, he was looking right at me.

"You're not just anyone."

The look in his eye took my breath away. He was still stern and intense, but the warmth in his hazel eyes turned hotter. It was wonderful to have Cole Townsend look at me like that, but it wasn't right.

"Please just charge me," I said softly. "I don't deserve any special treatment. You're the sheriff of the whole town and I'm a delinquent."

"You're not a delinquent."

I held up a hand to count out my crimes. "Possession of an illegal substance, trespassing, attempted breaking and entering, intent of theft—"

"What were you going to take?"

"Scrap metal. It's just sitting there and...Mr. Roberts always let me take it. Said it wasn't worth the hassle of selling. So I'd take it down and keep the money." I took a deep breath. I'd never admitted to myself the fact that my boss probably knew how much the metal was worth, but wanted me to have the money. He let me keep my pride by earning it.

"And now that he fired you, you can't." The pity in his

face made me want to crawl into a hole. He put his hand on my shoulder. "It's going to be okay."

I laughed because I didn't know what else to do. He sounded so sure of himself.

"You trust me right?"

I gazed into his hazel eyes. *Of course I trust you.* The words sat on the tip of my tongue. My stomach growled.

"I'm going to make you some food." He stood, and my body cried out at the loss of his warm weight. "Shower first. I bet you're ready to get out of those clothes."

"Why, Cole, I thought you'd never ask."

He glared. "You're wet and cold, and coming down from a high. I'm going to get you something dry to wear, and you're going to wash up. You're filthy."

I huffed. He didn't have to say it like that.

He led me to a little bathroom. The ranch house wasn't much to look at from the outside but inside everything looked clean and new.

"This is nice tile," I said as if I was getting a tour. "Who did it?"

"I did." Cole said. "I fix this place up on my days off."

Of course he did.

He turned on the shower and tested the water. "In you go. Help yourself to soap and shampoo."

"You're not going to wash my back?" I snarked. The thought of a simple creature comfort like hot water brought my courage back.

"Not unless you need me to." He raised a brow, as if waiting for me to be a smart aleck. Goddamn Cole Townsend. Even when he was twelve he'd had the ability to make me feel about two feet tall. When I said nothing, he nodded and left. The bathroom door clicked decisively behind him.

I stripped. I had to get out of this mess. My mom would be okay for the night—her nurse was there, but if she woke in the morning and I was still gone, she'd be worried sick. If she remembered who I was.

My best bet for escape was a high window which was at the end of the tub—a sign that this house was old enough to originally have a claw foot tub. If I stood on the tub's edge, I could peer out at the rainy night, but the old frame seemed to be painted shut. I worked at it for a minute and got it to budge when the bathroom door opened.

"Regina?"

I froze.

"I'm just taking your wet things to the wash."

"Okay!" I waited until the door closed again before cussing. There went my escape plan.

I hit the window frame and it shuddered free of the stuck paint. Maybe I could jimmy it open and escape in a towel.

A few minutes later, I'd gotten the window open enough to get my front half through. Rain slicked down the front lawn ahead of me. If I wedged my feet on the tub's edge, I could get enough height to push myself through.

I was about to retreat and wrap myself in a towel so I could attempt a jailbreak when the window fell onto my shoulders, pinning me. I yelped. In my struggle, my feet slipped off their tenuous perch on the side of the tub.

Panicking, I barely heard the bathroom door open.

"You okay in there?"

"Fine!" I answered before I realized he'd be able to tell my head was sticking out of the house. For a second I thought he bought it, when a rustle and a waft of air on my bare back told me Cole had drawn the shower curtain back.

"Regina…"

"I was just seeing how hard it was raining," I said. My feet had found purchase on the side of the tub again, but one move and they might slip. "You know, you really should replace these windows. I'm stuck."

Cole said nothing.

I was acutely aware of my bare naked buns pointing at him. The water of the shower was turning cold, not to mention the rain on my face. He needed to replace his gutters, too.

"A little help here?" I demanded.

Cole turned off the water. He laid a hand on my back and slid it down the curve of my ass. Probably inspecting his handiwork from before. The sting had subsided to a dull throbbing ache that I barely noticed until his fingers squeezed lightly. Despite myself I shivered, hard, and not because it was cold. After all the liberties he'd taken that night, blistering my bottom, this soft touch made everything inside me quiver to attention.

"You know," he said. "This isn't a bad position. Maybe I should leave you here all night."

I opened my mouth to yell at him and thought better of it. "Please don't."

Already the warmth from the shower was dissipating, and I'd started to shiver with real cold.

The hand left my backside to push the window up. I bit my lip as his body pressed against me.

"Careful." His heat hit my back as he helped me down. He set me on my feet and checked me over, while I looked anywhere but his face. He'd changed into jeans and a faded white t-shirt. His feet were bare. That seemed strangely intimate.

Naked, wet and cold, I stared at the washed out logo on his t-shirt. I didn't have it in me to be a smart aleck.

"Turn around."

Using a washcloth, he rubbed marks from the window off my back. I didn't speak as he took my hand, toweled me off like I was seven years old. To be honest, I'd been acting like it.

"Time to dress you, sweetheart."

Sweetheart? This was very un-sheriffy.

I hesitated.

"Put your hands up," he ordered. That was more like it.

I did and he dropped the t-shirt over my head, whipping the towel away at the same time. The soft fabric went to my knees. I forgot how big he was. Big and broad and suddenly the bathroom was too small for the two of us.

"Cole. What are you doing?"

"I'm taking care of you." He bound up my wet hair, then gave the pony tail a tug. "Come on."

4

minute later, I sat in his little kitchen drinking a glass of water and studying the wallpaper.

"Cole."

"Yes?" He didn't turn from the counter.

"Your kitchen is decorated in tiny cocks."

"Roosters."

"Whatever. I guess the renovations haven't made it this far."

"Maybe I just like chickens," he said mildly, setting a sandwich on a plate and glass of milk in front of me.

My eye followed the march of red-combed birds around his entire kitchen. "No one likes chickens this much."

"Eat." He tapped the plate. "You need it."

I finally looked him in the eye.

Straight nose, short buzzed hair that somehow looked soft as down. Hazel eyes. Delicious mouth. I was in Cole Townsend's house, he'd seen my bare butt twice, and we were all alone.

I shivered.

He frowned. "I'll turn the heat up."

I picked up the sandwich. To my delight, it had peanut butter and white marshmallow fluff together on sensible wheat bread.

"A Fluffernutter," I breathed in awe. "Where did you find the fluff?"

"Cross Brothers grocer still has it. You told me Fluffernutters are your favorite."

A thrill went through me that he remembered.

"You told me I shouldn't eat them."

"It's pure sugar." He winced. "You don't need anything to make you more hyper."

I grinned. "That was the last summer you worked as a camp counselor. I knew I had something to do with it."

"Yes, Regina." He sighed. "All the camp counselors vowed to quit that day."

I ate while he watched me, an almost smile playing over that perfect mouth. I even drank the milk when he tapped the glass. My throat still felt dry.

I jumped when his radio crackled. He rose. "I need to take this." He pointed a finger at me. "Stay."

I nodded, happy to obey. Cole always had the power to make me stay put. Right now, I was enjoying the sound of his voice giving orders over the phone. So dominant and...sheriff-y.

The call ended and he strode back. "Finish your sandwich, Regina."

"Okay." I obeyed like I was six again, and he was twelve. He watched me while I ate, and I loved it now as I loved it then.

"You look good, Cole. Very official."

"Glad you approve."

I started to speak with my mouth full, but he fixed me with a glare and I chewed.

"We're going to talk more in the morning, but tell me this...why didn't you ask for money?"

The delicious combo of peanut butter and marshmallow cream turned to dust in my mouth. "Who would I ask?" I made myself swallow. My heart hurt.

"Regina."

"No, who Cole? My trailer park neighbors? My college friends, who've just graduated with a ton of loans? My dad, who walked out when I was ten?" I hunched my shoulders and pushed the plate away. "I'm done."

He put the plate in the sink, and returned and put his hand on mine on the table. "You could've said something."

I scoffed. I couldn't help it. I'd never fit in and he knew it.

He sat back, looking disappointed. The sight tugged on my heartstrings. Did he really think I'd run to him? He'd looked after me a few times when we were kids, but I hadn't even spoken to him since I returned, forced to return home after only two years of college.

"We'll talk in the morning," he said. "After you've had a little sleep, you'll be thinking clearer."

"What makes you think I'm not thinking clearly now?"

"You tried to climb out of my bathroom window buck naked."

I scowled at the mental image. "I was going to take a towel."

He shook his head, but there was a little smile around the corner of his mouth. "You're not a mean drunk. You're a hilarious one. But I think it's best you sleep this off."

"I can walk home."

"You're not going anywhere."

"But my mom—"

"I called your house. Your mom's sleeping. Becky is

there, and has instructions to tell your mom you're with a friend, if she asks."

"You called my mother? You can't do that."

"Do what?"

"Take over my life!"

"Someone has to."

"What the hell does that mean?" Somehow Cole knowing my life was a mess was too much to bear.

He hesitated. "We'll talk in the morning."

"No, Cole, now."

"Mr. Roberts called me. He's worried about you."

"Because I missed a few days of work before he fired me?"

"That, and the fact that you stole over three grand from him in the past four months."

I felt hot. Then cold. Then numb. "How did you know?"

"He told me."

Denial was on my tongue, it tasted like dust. I swallowed it. My shoulders slumped in defeat.

"How did he find out?" My voice sounded tiny, like it was coming from very far away.

"You're not going to deny it?"

"No."

"Good girl," he murmured. The words made me feel better than I had all night. Weird.

"He checked a few strange shipments, orders for supplies never received. He realized you faked them."

I had. I wasn't proud of it. $400 here, $200 there. The largest was $700, and I forged a receipt in one of the warehouse bathrooms. I needed so much more. Mr. Roberts was a good man. He gave me my first job when I was sixteen, and took me back when I dropped out of college to look after my mom. I'd been desperate for a job, and he'd helped me out.

I was the worst person in the world.

"No, you're not," Cole said, and I realized I'd spoken aloud. "You messed up, but it's going to be okay."

"How can it possibly be okay?"

"Because I'm going to fix it." He tugged me up. "Come on. We're going to bed."

We?

"You need sleep."

I didn't resist until we were halfway down the hall.

"Wait, Cole. What do you mean you're going to fix it? Won't it seem weird that I'm in all this trouble, and then I'm here?"

"Relax, Regina, let me worry about it."

"Cole, no," I tugged my hand out of his.

I was swaying on my feet, so tired I could barely see. In the dim bedroom, his body filled my vision.

Gently, he maneuvered me to the bed, and tipped me over his lap.

Whap whap whap! His hand beat a strict tattoo. It didn't quite hurt, but I felt my buns heating up.

He rubbed my bottom and relaxation poured through me.

He set me on my feet, arms still around me to gently squeeze my plump cheeks.

"What was that for?"

"Remind you who's in charge." His voice was deep, so deep, like a pool I could fall into. My head nodded as I leaned into him.

His fingers stroked back my hair from my face. "You like it when I spank you?" He sounded curious, but heat lept into his hazel eyes.

"I don't not like it." I buried my embarrassed face into his chest, hoping he wouldn't push for a longer answer.

He let me, wrapping his arms around me and murmuring into my ear. "Now you're clean, warm, and fed. You're going to sleep and in the morning we're going to talk."

"Okay."

"Good girl."

Warmth spread through my whole body. Cole put me to bed and tucked his body around me. His heat seeped into my body, and even exhausted, I felt higher than I'd been all night. I was in handsome Cole Townsend's bed, bum hot from my three spankings, my body practically trembling with lust as the big man of my dreams spooned me. I wasn't sure how the events of the night had brought me to this, but I'd take it.

I'd think about my problems in the morning.

I WOKE in the middle of the night, absolutely parched.

"Cole—" I coughed.

His arms wrapped around me in a vice grip. I felt hot, too hot.

"Regina?"

"Water," I croaked.

He was out of bed in a shot, padding to the kitchen.

I sat up the instant his warmth receded and reality hit me.

I scrambled out of the bed and got the heck out of there.

I made it down the hall and to the door before strong arms wrapped around my body, pulling me back to the warm wall of Cole's bare chest.

"Whoa, where do you think you're going?"

"Let me go, Cole." I struggled.

"Let's get you back in bed."

He hoisted me easily and I kicked.

"Let me go! I have to go!"

He sat me on the bed and handed me the water. Despite my desire to escape, I drank greedily.

"Where do you have to go?"

"To check my mom."

"She's with the night nurse."

"Sometimes she wakes up though. Crying. And she always wants me." I didn't add that it was the only time she knew who I was.

He was silent while I finished the water.

"Do you want more?" he asked when I handed him the glass. I shook my head.

"Regina, do you wake up every night like this? Even when you were working?"

"Sometimes. Well, most nights, yes."

"All right." He sighed, sounding tired. "Let's call Becky."

"Becky?"

"The night nurse. I spoke with her earlier."

I felt a little guilty because Cole sounded so tired. But I figured as a sheriff he was used to calls in the middle of the night.

Becky came on the line, sounding way more chipper than anyone had a right to be at 3 am. She assured me all was well.

"Does that make you feel better?" Cole asked as he ended the call.

"A little. No," I started up, "I need to get home. Becky leaves at 7, and I need to arrange for someone to be there so I can find a job—"

Once again, Cole caught me and pulled me to the bed. "Enough. It's the middle of the night. You need sleep."

"But Cole—" I struggled, sleep-fogged and upset. I really was tired.

"Enough. Keep this up and I'll handcuff you to the bed," he said in a firm enough tone that I believed him. "We'll get to your mom's house in time, I promise. Right now you need to rest."

"I'm all she has," I protested.

"Not with Becky there. She's trained to take care of her. If she hadn't answered the phone, I'd have driven over there, but she answered. Your mom is sleeping, she's fine."

"I'm up now. I don't want to sleep," I said between yawns.

He sighed. Two seconds later I was face down over his lap.

"What are you doing?" I shrieked as he pulled up my nightshirt.

"Getting you to sleep."

"Cole! That's not going to work!"

"It worked before." He kneaded my buns, and started swatting. "Spanking releases endorphins."

"Did you read that in the police manual?"

"Hush," he said firmly. His palm smacked one butt cheek, then the other, spreading the sting evenly over my quivering flesh.

It did calm me.

When he set me on my feet, I swayed drunkenly.

"Why are you doing this?"

I could've misheard him, but I swear he whispered, "Because you're mine."

5

Morning came and I woke. I got out of bed, but delayed leaving the room until I really had to pee.

The sight of me in the mirror, bruises under my eyes and hair a mess, made me cringe. Had I really said all those things last night? Done them?

I lifted the shirt Cole gave me to wear and checked my backside. Sure enough, there was some lingering redness.

So it wasn't a dream.

I padded back to the bedroom and looked for a clock. There had been one on the bedside table, but it was gone. Light streamed through the curtains.

I hit the kitchen in a panic.

Cole leaned against the counter, sipping coffee and reading a paper. My body jolted to a stop at the sight of his long legs encased in jeans, a black polo taut on his muscled biceps and chest.

"Morning, sunshine," he said.

"What time is it?" I demanded, and pointed to the microwave that said ten am. "Is that right?"

"Yes."

"Goddammit, Cole!"

"Regina," his voice crackled with authority. "Relax. I called and asked for a day nurse to come. Your mother is up and fine. The new nurse is Matthew. She calls him Peter, but the nurse told me that's normal."

"Peter is her brother. He's been dead twenty years."

"Well, she's having a good conversation with him. Now come sit. We have things to talk about."

I crept to the table, keeping my eyes on Cole. He looked rested and handsome, not a hair out of place.

Bastard.

I felt like my eye sockets were filled with cotton. I told Cole this when he asked how I was doing.

"How's your rear end?" he asked. "Sore?"

"No."

"Bruises?"

"No. Was that your goal? To bruise my butt?"

He raised a brow at my tone. "If it'll teach you not to get in the car with Benny again."

My turn to raise a brow. "You really don't like him."

"If you knew what I knew, you wouldn't either."

"I don't need to know anything more to dislike him. Not like Donnie DeMarco," I mentioned my long ago ex-boyfriend, who I was pretty sure now worked for the mob.

Sure enough, Cole glowered.

"Never mind." I took a sip of coffee, and kept my eyes on the table. "We need to talk."

"We do. How much do you remember from last night?"

"All of it. You know everything I've done. You caught me doing most of it, and the rest Mr. Roberts told you."

"So that's it?" His gaze was hard.

"Yes."

"Well, then you have two options." He set the coffee cup down. "One is I take you down to the station, charge you. I'll ask Mr. Roberts to press charges, and he will. You'd be wise to plead guilty. The judge would sentence you. You might get some jail time. Your mom will go to a nursing home—"

"What's the second option?" I interrupted.

He fixed me with a stern look and continued. "The second option is unique, but you won't like it any more. There's no jail time, no reporting the crime. Mr. Roberts trusts me to handle it, and I said I'd do my best. It's up to you, though."

I wanted to know what option two entailed, but couldn't help asking, "Why would he do that? Why would he tell you everything and ask you for help?"

"Because he knows I care about you. When you got back from college, I checked in on you from time to time."

"You did?"

"Yes. I would've gone to you directly, but ever since the rock incident, I knew you weren't speaking to me."

"The rock incident?" I asked, startled. Then I remembered. "Oh yeah." When I was fourteen, and hanging with a crowd slightly older, some people thought it would be cool to sit at an overpass and throw rocks at cop cars. I wasn't involved, until I heard that Cole had caught some of them, but the only kid who got in trouble was the one who lived in the trailer park. I'd been reading Malcolm X, and went and screamed at Cole for discrimination.

"I called you a racist."

"It was unfortunate that the only kid I caught with a rock in his hand was Winston. And that the driver only accused him of throwing rocks, and not the white kids."

"You made an example of him. I didn't think it was fair."

"It wasn't fair," Cole said, surprising me. "I wanted to

charge all of them as delinquents. The sergeant wouldn't let me. I decided that day to become sheriff."

I blinked in surprise.

"But Winston did okay," Cole continued. "The group home was better than his family home."

"Yeah," I said, thinking of how glad I would've been to escape my home when I was fourteen.

"But you weren't speaking to me."

"I thought you were one of them."

"One of who?"

"One of the people who think anyone who lives in a trailer park is trash."

"I never thought that, Regina."

"Your parents did."

"That's why I never told them the real reason I volunteered at the day camp."

My eyes widened at the insight. In addition to his brief stint as a camp counselor, Cole had worked as a lifeguard at the lake where I spent summers in a state run outdoor activity program. He'd never gotten close, but I'd spent many a summer playing under his watchful eye.

It hit me then that Cole had always looked out for me, even when I gave him hell.

"I'm sorry," I said. "I was rude to you a lot. You must have wanted to spank me for a long time."

His eyes darkened. "You have no idea."

I shivered again. It was becoming a habit around Cole. Like my body knew there was something more going on under the surface. We'd known each other so long, and always shared a connection. It was deeper, more visceral, somehow, now that we'd grown up. But our relationship was comfortable, familiar. Deep down, I'd always known that Cole was on my side.

"Well, then, what do you want me to do? Community service?"

"Something like that."

"Just spit it out, Cole." I crossed my arms in front of my chest, and his look grew even more stormy.

"Come here, Regina."

"Why?"

"Do as I say."

I stood, and took leaden steps until I stood between his legs.

"Good girl. Was that so hard?"

"Yes."

"You're going to have to get used to it. This is option two."

"Option two is you ordering me to get between your legs? Because I could be good with that."

"Regina."

"Sorry. I guess I don't get it."

"I want you to submit to me."

The tingles spread through my body again at the intense heat in Cole's eyes. I kept my face neutral. "Oh, is that all?"

"Option number two is you submit to my discipline. All day, every day. I'll tell you what to do, and you obey, no questions asked. Not only that, I'm going to control everything. Your schedule, what you wear. There are some orders I'll give you that will be general, like instructing you to eat three healthy meals a day, and others will be more specific. But if you choose option two, you'll follow them all."

I opened my mouth. Closed it. I'd known Cole was a control freak, but this gave it a whole new meaning.

"We'll communicate. You'll get to express yourself. I want you to be honest with me. And I have nothing but your highest good in mind. You can trust me."

I still didn't know what to say. "You want to tell me what to do? Don't you already do that?"

A hint of a smile. "I want you to obey me."

"You want me to obey you," I repeated slowly. Unaccountably, my pussy moistened.

"You will be accountable to me. I will keep you in line, and if you step out of line..."

"You'll spank me."

"Among other forms of discipline, yes."

I stared at him, waiting for him to crack a smile and tell me it was all a joke. But who was I kidding? This was Cole. He didn't joke.

"You really mean this."

"I've never been more sincere about anything in my life."

"What if you tell me to do something crazy, like jump off a bridge or something?"

"Regina, you know me. Would I ever allow you to do something that brings you harm?"

He had a point.

"Your current life choices haven't been positive. So, I'll be making them for you."

"For how long?"

"As long as I deem necessary."

"So...option one is prison, and option two is you control my life so it feels like I'm in prison."

"You may enjoy some parts of it more than prison. Some parts less. All's it will cost you is your pride."

I scowled. "I like my pride. It's all I have left."

"And look where it got you. I said I was going to help you. This is how."

"So you're going to mold me into the perfect citizen. Using the carrot and the stick method."

"Mostly the stick. Unless you're a very, very good girl."

I ignored the tingles spreading through me. "I've read about this," I said. "What's my safeword...prison?"

"It can be."

I stared. "Shit. You really are a sadist."

"I have never once spanked a woman before last night. Not even by her request." He grinned, startling me. "I never would've guessed you'd respond so well."

I squirmed and his grin darkened a shade.

I exhaled. "Okay. So I do what you say, and I don't have to go to jail?"

"It's not going to be easy, Regina. I have high standards, and I expect you to follow the rules. Or you'll be punished."

"Are you trying to talk me out of this?"

"Yes."

"Well, it won't work. I'll do exactly what you say, when you say it."

His eyes glittered. "Good." He leaned back. "Take the coffee cups, wash them, and put them in the dishwasher."

I hesitated. His eyebrow went up.

This was a test. He thought I'd balk? I'd call his bluff.

I started to obey, but couldn't keep from grumbling. "You have a dishwasher, I don't understand why I have to rinse them first."

Cole's heat hit my back as he crowded me to the counter.

"Lesson one," he breathed into my ear, and every nerve in my body got a thrill. "You do as ordered, without complaining."

"But I'm so good at it," I complained. "Snark is my life. I eat sarcasm for breakfast."

"I know." His body pressed against mine, forcing me to lean over the sink. "Put your hands on the counter."

I did, gripping the edge of the sink so he wouldn't see how they shook with excitement.

"You're going to learn to behave, if I have to beat it into you." He used his feet to urge mine apart.

"You're spanking me because I whined?"

"No." His whisper tickled my ear. "I'm spanking you because I can." He pulled my hips back and folded my nightshirt up.

"Push your bottom out. I want a good target." I did, now as excited as he sounded. My pussy was liable to drip on the floor.

A giddy feeling swept through me. "Point your toes in. You won't be able to clench your bottom."

"Does that make it hurt more?" I asked. Trust Cole to study this sort of thing.

The first blow rocked me forward onto my hands. I sucked in a breath. That hurt more than the last two spankings he'd given me.

"You tell me."

He continued peppering my bottom. I breathed through it, my eyes watering. Still, being disciplined by a hot guy beat going to lock up any day.

He finished, squeezing my bottom. The rough massage cut the sting in half. My own hands itched to clutch my bottom.

"Now go stand in the corner. Nose to the wall and use both hands to hold up your shirt."

The fresh pain warned me to obey. As I stared at the wall, I heard him move around the room behind me.

This was crazy. I was standing in the corner with my red ass on display like a child caught with her hand in the cookie jar, while Cole sat at the kitchen table and watched. I wasn't sure what was worse—the pain or the humiliation.

My pussy was so very wet.

"Regina, come here."

This time I couldn't keep from blushing as I stood in front of him. He studied me. Even seated, he was a hair taller. "You still want to do this?"

I nodded.

"Bend over the table." He indicated the spot right beside him. Whimpering, I did and he lifted the shirt I wore, inspecting his work.

I sucked in a breath as he palmed my ass, but he only put the shirt down and let me rise to face him.

"So that's it?" I tried to sound nonchalant, even though I wanted to beg him to take me to the bedroom and ravish me.

He nodded. "Most discipline will hurt but won't mark you, though I intend to give you a good paddling for stealing. You'll think twice before doing it ever again."

I shifted from foot to foot, thinking.

He stilled me. "Just relax, and trust me. Tell me what you're thinking."

"This is all very strange," I blurted.

"Unorthodox. But it's the way things are going to be, unless you want the law involved."

"I don't want the law involved," I said absently. My hand went to rub my bottom and he caught it, and gave me a chastising look.

"Okay. I don't have a job any more, so what am I going to be doing all day? Will I be able to see my mom?"

"You will have set times to see your mom. I'm not going to keep you from her, obviously, but I think you need some time away from her, and you won't allow yourself to take it. So, I'm ordering you to do it. You'll have no choice." His fingers curled around my hip. "Same with keeping to a healthy sleeping and eating schedule."

"Okay. What else?"

"Counseling for starters. There's a group that meets Mondays in the church."

"I know you don't believe me, but I don't drink or smoke pot on a regular basis." I tensed. "I don't need counseling."

"It's not for addiction. It's for caregivers."

I pulled my hand out of his. "Cole—"

"This is non-negotiable." His words may as well have been carved in stone. "You'll also spend a set amount of time volunteering. A way of paying your debt to society. I'll put some thought to where."

"The police station?"

"Not there, or any place I have jurisdiction over. You'll be spending a lot of time over here, and people will assume favoritism."

"They'd be right. What am I going to do here?"

"Whatever I want." His other hand grasped my hip. My pussy started throbbing.

"What do you want?" I whispered.

"A maid for one. And three square meals a day. You can cook, right?"

My mouth dropped open.

"If not, I can get some cookbooks from the library. If you mess up, I'll spank you. That should be good incentive." A smile played around his mouth, I knew he was joking. About the spanking at least.

"I can cook." I brushed his hands away. "You sexist pig, if you think—"

He turned me to the table and delivered three quick swats to my ass. I yelped. He turned me back to face him and continued as if he hadn't been interrupted.

"I'm glad you can cook. I expect at least a sandwich for lunch and something hot for dinner. You may end up putting one or two of my meals in the fridge. I work long hours. You'll be making food for yourself, too."

"This is unbelievable. You expect me to cook for you—"

"And clean. I assume you know how to do that. If not, you'll have to learn quick."

"This isn't punishment...this is slavery!"

"A little bit. I could get used to having you as my slave, naughty one." He pinched my bottom.

I slapped his hand. "What the hell, Cole!"

"Language. I think we'll add a rule: no swearing, or I'll soap your mouth."

I opened my mouth to scream and thought about it. Cole was offering me a way out. Not just of my crimes, but of my shitty life. I'd dropped out of college to take care of my mom, and spent the last two years working as much as I could and still stressing about money. The state provided some funds for my mom's home nurse, but there was still a hefty deductible. The reason I'd stolen was I was swimming in bills, with no way out. It'd be nice to unplug and not think about my problems for a while.

Still. "I can't believe this. It's...just...insane."

"No, what's insane is that a young woman with her whole future ahead of her allows herself to get run down and broke caring for her mother, and so starts stealing from her longtime employer and talking to a druggie with a thought to sell. I've watched you grow up and I won't let you throw your life away. You're too important."

Again, he mentioned me being special to...someone. Him?

"I didn't know what else to do. Home care is expensive."

"What about a full time facility? The state will cover the cost—"

"No." I raised my voice. "I'm not putting her in a facility."

There were tears in my eyes. "All we can afford is the state one. I visited. There was no air conditioning, and the residents looked like they wanted to die. Some of them already seemed dead. There were flies on them, and no one cared enough to swat them off." I scrubbed my aching eyes with a hand, fighting back tears. "I'm not doing it." My voice sounded broken, even to me.

"All right." Cole's hands returned to my hips, giving me a squeeze.

"I won't abandon her. Dad already did. That's not who I am."

"You're right. It's not who you are. You'd rather steal than lose your pride. I don't approve of it, but I understand. And so does Mr. Roberts."

"What?"

"He says you can keep the money."

"I can never see him again," I whispered. "I wouldn't be able to look him in the eye."

He squeezed my hips again. "It's okay, sweetheart. I'll help you fix it. I promise."

"How?"

"We'll get to that," he said, and rose. "I am going to help you."

I SPENT the rest of the day trying to wrap my head around the deal I'd made with Cole. After breakfast, he gave me back my now clean clothes, and we hopped in his truck and headed to my mom's house.

My mom sat at the table, eating cheerios like a toddler. She didn't respond to me at all.

Matthew, the day nurse, was charming, however.

My mother's trailer was worn, but I kept it clean at least. Cole's eyes darted around the space, missing nothing. My face grew hot when I compared my home to the stately brick house Cole had grown up in. His parents lived in a neighborhood that was the Who's Who of Licking Hole-doctors, lawyers, businessmen. Mine had a break-in or domestic disturbance every other night.

Cole caught my arm as I went to my bedroom to change. "Pack a bag," he said. "Enough for a few nights."

That was easy. I didn't have many clothes. I stopped in the bathroom and changed into a short skirt and a shirt fitted to my breasts. I even swiped on some mascara and stared at myself in the mirror.

"Slut," I mouthed to the image.

Who was I fooling? I couldn't pretend I didn't want him. I pressed my hands to my cheeks as if I could wipe the blush away.

My short skirt and cleavage told me I knew exactly what I was doing. After all these years, I had my escape plan. It may only be temporary, and it was a little weird, but Cole had finally come to my rescue. I'd spent every waking minute of my childhood trying to get away from this place, and now I had a way out.

Drawing confidence around me like a cloak, I flounced out. Cole took in my outfit with a sweep of his eyes. He didn't say anything, but I noticed his lips pressed together a moment before he spoke.

"Ready to go?"

"Yes." I kissed my mom's cheek and hit the door, muttering, "Get me out of here."

~

On the car ride home, I searched Cole's face for any sign of what he was thinking. He had to be disgusted by my family home. He'd always looked out for me, but he'd made it clear we didn't belong together.

Once, a group of boys decided to pick on me at the local swimming hole. I was twelve, my breasts had come in early, and I was starting to attract all sorts of attention. Cole used to lifeguard at the beach, but it was just a coincidence he was there that day when my tormentors surrounded me. With a word and look, Cole sent the boys packing, and I had my hero back again.

I stepped close to hug him, but he stiffened and moved away.

"You need to be careful, Regina," he said.

I glowered. I hadn't asked for the stupid breasts. "Whatever, Cole," I said. He was eighteen, a new recruit in the police academy. Girls had mourned when he shaved off his blond hair, but I loved the short, pale buzz. I wanted to run my hands over it, see if it was as soft as it looked.

To test him, I took a step forward, and he retreated, looking away as if my presence pained him.

He was still the good, golden boy, and I was a little dark-eyed girl from the wrong side of the tracks.

"I hate you anyway. You're just as bad as the rest of them."

That was the last time Cole stuck up for me. I wondered what had changed.

I slumped in my seat as Cole's truck idled at a stoplight. God forbid someone on the sidewalk see us together.

"This is never going to work," I muttered to the truck window.

"What's that, Regina?"

"I said, what about work?"

"What about it?"

"Well, I need money, you know, to pay bills."

"I'll handle it."

"Cole." I braced my hands on the dash and stared him down until he transferred his eyes from the traffic light to me.

"I said I'll handle it. I think you need a break. I'll make sure you're covered until the end of the month, and then we'll reassess."

My forehead crinkled. This was serious. I could handle spankings and crazy sexual tension, but don't mess with my money. "How long is this going to last?"

"As long as it takes," he said, a muscle jumping in his cheek.

I thumped the dash. "That's not an answer."

"As long as we want," he said, hoarsely, and we weren't just talking about the deal.

"Is this a good idea?" I asked quietly. We still were dancing around where this arrangement was headed, and I was fine with that. I liked to dance. But I wasn't willing to risk fucking up real things, like rent and bills, for a fling with my long time crush.

He glared ahead at the road. "How do you mean?"

"You're risking a lot for me."

He didn't answer.

I cast about for another reason. "Do you really want people to see me with you?"

"Why would I care about that?"

Was he serious? One look at me, and his WASP parents would freak. Men like Cole did not date Reginas. They dated women like Lucy Litt, and had pretty blond babies who went to Sunday School.

Who was I kidding? Cole and I weren't dating. This was

a blackmail situation, even if it did involve sex. He wouldn't be taking me home to his parents.

I sighed. "Never mind. So you'll handle the bills. I'll stay at your house and cook and clean. Play house like your little wifey." I glanced over to see if he liked the sound of that.

"Good," he said neutrally as we pulled back into his driveway. "It'll keep you out of trouble."

AT THE HOUSE, Cole made me sit down and tell him all my bills. There was a lot more red than black on some of them.

I tallied what I owed Mr. Roberts on a separate sheet.

Cole looked it over while I tried to hide my tears.

He noticed them anyway. "You didn't want to steal from him."

"I had to. They were going to take mom out of the program, if I didn't pay the minimum deductible."

"It never occurred to you to ask for help?"

"There was no one to ask."

"Mr. Roberts?"

"He'd already given me enough."

"Someone in the community, then?"

"I hadn't been to church in a long while. I wasn't really welcome there."

"There had to be someone."

"No." I stared at my lap. Did I really need to explain that my family wasn't like his? We didn't have money or connections or invites to the annual Policeman's Ball, a small but powerful gathering of the Who's Who of Licking Hole.

Cole pulled out a handkerchief (of course, he had a handkerchief) and wiped my eyes. I felt truly broken.

"Someday," he murmured, "you're going to realize you're worth helping."

"Cole...what am I going to do?"

"I'm going to help you. But you're going to do everything —and I mean everything—I say."

He took a few calls and came back to me wringing my hands.

"This isn't going to work. You, me—I don't even know what you want from me."

"Shhh, baby. One thing at a time." His hand on the back of my neck quieted me. It made me feel submissive and safe at the same time. "Just relax and do as I say. Don't think. Just think about how to please me."

"Pleasing you?" My breath caught. My real concern about this arrangement was how much I wanted him. He wanted me to cook and clean for him? Fine I'd do it, gladly. Because being around him made my head swim. I wasn't sure how long I could go before I screamed, "just do me, already." Or waited until he came home one night and jumped his bones.

Working around him would be impossible. There weren't enough changes of underwear in the world.

"I don't know what to think about all this."

"Then don't think. Just be." He massaged my neck. "Thinking is what got you in this mess. You think too much. Not that you shouldn't think...I love how intelligent you are. But your mind is going in circles and needs a break." His hand rubbed circles over my back. "Now calm down. I have to go to the station for a while. Are you going to sit tight and be good for me?"

I nodded.

"Good girl." Cole kissed my forehead. Entirely unsatis-factory, but I'd take it.

God, I was so in love with this man.

"First, I'm going to test your obedience. Go to the bedroom and put on the clothes I laid out for you."

Annoyance curled through me, but I told myself I'd signed on for this.

"Bossypants," I muttered under my breath as I headed to the bedroom. I was curious to see what sort of clothes Cole wanted me to wear.

"Oh, hell no." I lifted the flimsy black and white dress. It was a French maid outfit, complete with frilly apron.

I heard Cole behind me. He'd followed me, anticipating a tantrum.

"No," I said. "No, no, no." The fabric was silky and fine, but there wasn't much of it. The outfit came with silky panties and sexy black heels. My pussy clenched at the thought of wearing something so enticing for Cole, but my pride overruled it. "No, Cole. Just no."

"Hush." He caught my chin in two fingers and held me still. The gesture sent tremors of submission through me. "You will wear this dress because I want it, and you belong to me."

"Is this some sort of sick fantasy I play into?"

"Maybe. But you're going to do what I want, when I want. You may not like all of it, but you can trust me. You know that." He released me. "Say 'prison' and you can go. Otherwise, change."

I threw the outfit on the bed. "This is so wrong."

"So is a beautiful, intelligent young woman throwing her whole life away because she's too proud to ask for help."

"You don't understand, Cole. All I have is my pride."

"Not anymore. I'm going to take your pride. And give you something more."

"What's that?"

"Peace." He took the outfit from me and folded it carefully. "You don't have to think, or worry. I'm taking care of all it, sweetheart. It's going to be hard, but you can do it. I believe in you. Now get dressed, little maid." He swatted my rear as he headed towards the door. "My house isn't going to clean itself."

I growled to myself as I changed. I felt two things: the acute curl of humiliation suspiciously located in my groin, and a resigned agreement to what he said. My life was a mess. If he was volunteering to fix it...well, the jury was still out on that. Until then, I'd dress up like his sex dream and pretend things were all right.

There were worse fates than living out Cole's fantasies.

The outfit fit perfectly. The top smoothed over my bust and left my back bare. The skirt was a joke, but the sky-high heels made my usually dumpy legs look longer. I stood in front of the full-length mirror, smoothing the fabric over my curves.

I was nervous. Nervous to meet Sheriff Sadist and his pervy fantasy. But I wanted him to like what he saw.

I wanted to please him.

That thought annoyed me most of all.

Gritting my teeth, I put it all on. My breasts almost spilled out, but I supposed that was the point. After ten years of trying to cover up my huge breasts, wearing baggy t-shirts in summer and carefully picking necklines for work, it was a relief to flaunt my curves.

I peeked in the full-length mirror. Holy hotness. The costume looked amazing with my hourglass figure. All the doubt I had washed away when I realized I was in Cole's house wearing a sexy outfit by his request. Nay, by his order.

Beat the hell outta doing time.

Inspired, I swiped on some more mascara and smudged some eyeliner for a foxy look. "Here goes nothing."

I clopped back into the kitchen. Cole was across the room on the phone, his tall form silhouetted in light coming through the window. I caught my breath at his broad shoulders, his body lean but obviously muscular. The long legs, the taut waist. His trim form filled out the sheriff's uniform perfectly—and I usually ran at the sight of uniforms. It helped that under the standard issue black trousers was a perfect ass.

He turned slightly and I admired his profile—the strong jaw, the patrician nose. There was a reason the townspeople voted him sheriff at the tender age of twenty-eight. He had an air about him that said: "Trust me. I'm a leader." It also said, "Cross me at your peril." Cole Townsend was the total package.

When he caught sight of me, he did a double take. I stepped out of the hall, tugging on the skirt as if it could somehow lengthen and cover more of me.

Striding into the kitchen, he signaled me to twirl. My gut clenched, but so did my pussy.

I pirouetted, teetering a little on the heels.

His face when I finished was a wonder.

"I'll call you back," he said, and ended the call. Cocking his head, he looked me up and down.

"I think it fits okay." My face felt red.

The heat in his eyes told me how well it fit.

He advanced and I had the wild idea to back away from his predatory look.

My cheeks flushed as he loomed over me, not a hand's breath between us. Reaching down, he tugged at my outfit, straightening it. Hands at my side, I let him.

"You're beautiful, Regina. Relax." His hands held me carefully.

"I feel exposed."

"It's just me." He smiled, and my breath left me in a whoosh. I hadn't realized I was holding it. He continued turning me this way and that, admiring the black satin over the swell of my breasts and ass. "You should wear this all the time."

"Are you going to make me?"

"Maybe," he said, almost thoughtful. "It really does suit you."

I stuck my tongue out at him.

He tweaked my nose. "None of that. Do that again and I'll make you do chores with a clothespin on your tongue."

"Is that what I'm going to be doing? Chores?"

"What else?" His eyebrows raised, as if daring me to argue.

I sighed and kept my mouth shut.

He showed me the closet of cleaning supplies. "I have to go into work, but you can get started." He handed me a duster. "Clean from top to bottom, so you don't shake dust on what you've already—"

"I know how to clean." I gripped the duster like it was a sword, and imagined stabbing him with it.

He nodded slowly. Then, with a hand on the back of my neck, he bent me over and swatted my bottom. Hard.

I yelped. "What was that for?"

"Nothing," he said. "Just wanted to see how you look with a red handprint on your butt. And now I know."

He gathered his things and looked me up and down one more time. I didn't put up a fuss. A part of me felt I even deserved to be standing in the kitchen of my childhood crush, completely humiliated.

"Get cleaning."

∼

As I DUSTED, I took the opportunity to poke into Cole's personal things. Everywhere I looked, I found evidence that Cole was every bit of the fine, upstanding civil servant people believed him to be. The rooms were neat and clean, which made my job easier. Everything had a place from the tools in the mudroom to the neatly folded clothes in his dresser. There were no skeletons in any closet. I checked— twice. Even his garbage can was clean.

I was starting to suspect he wasn't human.

Giving up on dusting (as if dust dared to mar this perfect man's home), I caught a glimpse of myself in the full-length mirror. Exertion had brought color to my cheeks, but I still looked sleek and cool in the white lace and black satin. The fabric was soft to touch and made me ultra aware of my lush, feminine body.

It struck me that, in a twisted way, I was living my own fantasy as well as Cole's. Under different circumstances, tottering around the smoking hot sheriff's house dressed as a naughty maid could be the hottest thing I'd ever done.

Wait, it WAS the hottest thing I'd ever done.

My hands roamed over my body faster. I stroked my breasts, admiring their swell under the silky fabric. I turned and lifted the skirt to check out my ass, imagining pulling it up for Cole, showing off...

Now my face was bright with arousal. I sank onto the big bed and touched myself, imagining Cole's sleek body moving on top of me, the muscles in his shoulders bunching as he planted his arms on either side of my head. His eyes would pierce mine and he'd thrust...

I came in seconds, wet heat running over my hand.

"God," I gasped. One orgasm barely made a dent in my arousal.

I was hot and horny, and dressed like Cole's wet dream. He better come home soon, or I'd do something to make sure the sheriff made house calls.

Like set his house on fire.

Stomping through the house, I jabbed the duster into corners blindly. Horny desperation made me scowl.

Goddamn Cole. Who was this man, that he could degrade me so thoroughly, and make me enjoy it?

My only hope for escape was to find some piece of damning information, and blackmail him. There was a locked black box under his bed, and another, smaller one in the mudroom. I was no locksmith, so couldn't open them to find evidence of his kink. Whips, chains, floggers—even fluffy handcuffs...but there was nothing—besides the naughty maid costume. And I was wearing that, so technically I was the biggest evidence of Cole's kink.

There was no office, but a black laptop sat on an ottoman. Not standard police issue, so it must be Cole's personal one. I dusted around it.

His laptop tempted me. Did I really want to see a browser history full of fetish porn?

Answer: yes.

Damn thing had a password.

The front door opened and I scrambled up. How did he drive up so quietly?

He paused on the landing, his gaze sweeping around the house. Somehow, I knew he guessed what I'd been up to.

"Did you have an interesting time while I was away?"

"Yes," I steeled my shoulders. "You were in the running

for most freakishly neat man on the planet, but were disqualified because your spice cabinet isn't alphabetized."

"You can do that first thing tomorrow morning." His gaze settled on his laptop.

I squirmed, realizing I hadn't put it back where I found it. "I wanted to check my email."

He raised a brow but said nothing as he stalked to the laptop and typed in the password. His long fingers flew over the keys. He had beautiful hands, graceful and slender. I pretended I hadn't been staring when he turned the laptop to me.

Mollified by his trust, I went ahead and checked my email. I did snoop once he left the room to change clothes. The browser history was clear—someone had erased it recently—but there was a document saved to the desktop marked "Private."

I opened and found a list of chores, each assigned to a day.

Cole's hands settled on my shoulders and I jumped.

"I'd like you to stick to a schedule."

"'Kay," I said, a bit breathless from his close proximity. "Bathroom, kitchen...when am I to dust the dungeon? Or do you have your other slaves clean it?"

"No dungeon. No other slaves. You're my first." He played with the hair on the back of my neck, and every part of me stood at attention. Especially my clitoris. It was like I hadn't masturbated at all.

I closed the laptop. "Cole."

"Yes?"

"When are we going to...you know?" His elegant fingers stroked my neck, sending tremors through my body. I twisted to face him. "You're killing me here."

"Am I?"

"If I die of lust, it'll be manslaughter."

"Good luck getting a jury to convict me." His arms went around me and he nuzzled my neck.

"They'll convict you." His lips found my skin and I gasped under the sudden assault. "One look and they'll know you're a lady killer."

He kept kissing my neck, tugging the neckline aside to reveal my shoulder. I sighed and pressed back into him, awash with desire.

"Cole, please."

"Please, what, Regina?"

"Uh..."

"Use your words."

"I can't—"

I pivoted and pressed my mouth on his. He kissed me back, a hand coming up to knot in my hair. His lips were forceful and claiming.

Then he jerked my head back. "Enough," he said, and stood, leaving me wet and panting.

And bereft.

"Cole?" I stared at his straight back, the rigid line of his shoulders.

"Yes, Regina?"

I blinked back tears. This was more humiliating and painful than all the past twenty-four hours put together. "Do you not want me?"

His reaction was instantaneous. He turned and scooped me into his arms, settling back on the couch. "It's not that, sweetheart. You're beautiful."

"Then why—?" My breath caught as pain sliced through me. "Why would you make me do this, if you won't have sex with me?" My clit throbbed unhappily.

"Shhh, sweetheart," he said. "It's not you. It's me. I just want everything to be perfect."

"Do I please you?"

His arms tightened. "Yes, my god yes, you please me. You're all I ever wanted."

A huge weight lifted off of me. To go from secure, independent working woman to disheveled sex object should've been disconcerting, but somehow with Cole it wasn't. It was what I'd always wanted.

"Then why?"

"Because I want everything to be perfect. I want it to be right. I need things to be a certain way."

I sighed heavily. "Okay."

He gave me a little kiss, right below my ear. "You believe me?"

"I do. It hurts but...I trust you. You're the biggest control freak I know. You even fold your underwear."

"Not anymore. That's your job."

I let out a mock groan, breaking the serious mood, at least until he kissed me again, taking my breath away.

"Come on, little maid. Time for dinner."

I FELT Cole's eyes following me around the kitchen as I prepared dinner. He had a briefcase out and was looking over his papers, but every time I glanced at him, I caught him staring. I may have exaggerated the sway in my hips as I sashayed to and from the fridge and stove. I told myself it was just the high heels making me walk that way. I didn't want to admit how much I liked his attention.

He claimed he was attracted to me, and in this moment,

I felt it. We could cut the sexual tension with a knife. Could he not feel it?

Maybe he was a robot.

I grumbled as I cracked eggs into a bowl.

"What's that, Regina?"

"Nothing."

"What are you making?"

"Brinner. Breakfast for dinner. I inventoried your pantry and we don't have a lot of options."

"Make a list and I'll go shopping."

"You don't want to send me to the grocery store looking like this?" I gave a half curtsy. "The town thinks I'm crazy anyway. I'll tell them it's research for my psych degree."

"I don't want anyone looking at you but me."

"I'm used to it. I grew breasts when I was thirteen. Men noticed."

"I don't need to be reminded of that," he muttered.

Hmmm.

I turned back to the sausage frying in the pan. "Is that why you won't fuck me? Some sort of penance for lusting after me when I was underage?"

Goading him worked. He replaced his work papers and closed his briefcase with a snap.

"No. And watch your language. I won't tell you again."

He seemed frustrated. Good.

I set the plate down. "You can start eating. I'm not that hungry."

"You need to eat."

"I'm only hungry for one thing." I gave him a pointed look.

"Suit yourself," he said, and tucked in. Unbelievable. I was flouncing around his house like Mr. Walton's wet dream and Cole was ignoring me. Ignoring me! I stomped back to the skillet, hell bent on burning his eggs.

"Regina, I think those are done."

"Another minute." I headed to the pantry.

I returned to Cole waiting for me beside the stove, arms crossed over his chest as he glared at me. The burner was off, and a blue haze hung over the kitchen.

Perfect.

"Are you in the habit of leaving the stove while it's on?"

"Maybe. I get distracted."

He grabbed my wrist and pulled me to the kitchen table. I made him force me over his knees, gritting my teeth so I didn't cuss him out.

Drat. I didn't think this part of the plan through.

"I think you need a lesson in safety."

"You can't spank me for burning dinner!"

"I'm not going to spank you."

"Then why am I ass up over your lap?" A resounding smack on one cheek reminded me not to swear.

"Bottom up," I said hurriedly. "Derriere. Bum, rear, rump, buttocks, tuckus."

"Are you done?"

I thought a second. "Patootie."

"I'm not spanking you."

"You're not?"

"No." His hand roamed between my legs. "I'm giving you an orgasm."

"What!" I tried to rear up and strong hands held me in place. I could only kick my legs as he anchored my wrists in the small of my back. "This is not okay." At that moment, an orgasm via Cole seemed worse than a spanking.

"Shhhh." He ran his free hand up my thigh.

"Relax, Regina. Submit to me." Long, capable fingers

brushed over my panties. Slowly, oh, so slowly, one finger slipped under the gusset and stroked the wetness there.

"Cole." I jerked.

"Be still." He leaned on my back as his finger conducted a symphony around my clit, settling into the perfect spot.

I couldn't speak any more. I held my breath. Everything in my being focused on the feather-light touch.

"This is how I'm going to treat you," he said in a low, smooth voice. "Every time you act out, I'm going to give you what you need. It may be a spanking, it may be quiet time in the corner to think on what you've done." I whimpered, and thrashed a little, but he reaffirmed his hold of my wrists and pressed his arm against my back. His other hand never stopped the light, fluttering touch against my clit.

"I'm in control. I make the decisions. You comply. And whether you're good, or naughty, you are mine."

At the last phrase, everything in me clenched, and I orgasmed hard.

"Good girl." He rubbed circles on my bottom as I lay limp over his lap.

"Oh my god. That was...I think I drooled on your floor a little."

He released my wrists and helped me up. My body still tingled from his touch, and a part of me wanted to sink into his arms.

It was getting harder and harder to hate him.

"Feeling better?" he asked, setting me on my feet.

"Yes, sir."

He chuckled and chucked me under the chin. "I knew that would get you to mind."

"More," I breathed.

The world tilted as Cole upended me over his shoulder, and carried me in a fireman's hold to the bedroom. I kicked my legs happily until he set me down and I noticed he was scowling.

"Regina, did you make the bed this morning?"

"Yes," I defended myself. Of course, I'd rumpled things a little when I had happy time, but I wasn't about to tell him that.

I didn't need to. "You played with yourself." His long fingers smoothed over the coverlet.

I didn't know how he guessed these things, but I couldn't deny it. "So?" I went with brazen attitude. "I have needs."

Cole moved in a blur, and I ended up face down, half over his lap, half on the bed. My face pressed into the bed as he cupped between my legs.

"This is mine. Your orgasms are mine." His fingers, so gentle minutes ago, penetrated me, quick and hard. My body was primed so it didn't hurt, but I stilled. "You don't touch yourself without my permission. Do you understand me? Say *yes, sir.*"

"Yes, sir," I breathed.

"Good girl." His thumb brushed my clit, which was already standing up and begging for another orgasm, the slut. A few seconds of touching and my hips jerked, begging for more. He swatted the back of my thigh. "Did I say you could cum?"

"No, sir. It's just...you're good at this. Most men couldn't find their way to the clitoris with a GPS."

"Is that so?" He sounded amused. His fingers did another swirl over my sweet spot.

"God, yes." Another pass and he dipped a finger inside me. I went limp. He added fingers and fucked me with them until I shuddered apart yet again.

I still wanted more.

"Amazing. In the past ten minutes you've given me more orgasms than all my other lovers combined."

He chuckled and wiped his wet fingers on the back of my thigh. "I'm glad to be of service. What do you say?"

"More please."

Another slap, this one to my ass. "What about 'thank you'?"

"More like 'spank you'...ow!" I winced as he smacked me again, harder. "Thank you, thank you. Now will you fuck me?"

"No. Bedtime."

"What?" I raised my head to glance at the clock. "It's eleven pm!"

"We have to be up at four thirty."

"WE?!?"

"Yes. It's in your schedule."

I grouched as he made me brush my teeth and prepare for bed. Cole made these ordinary tasks thrilling somehow. His height, his scent, the way he leaned against the door watching me, his t-shirt riding up just enough for me to see a strip of hard muscled ab—his proximity alone turned me on like the most potent foreplay. By the time we got to bed, I was gagging for it.

"So we're sleeping together again? I thought last night was a one-time thing."

"I only have one bed."

"You know, if we're sleeping together...we may as just sleep together." I waggled my eyebrows.

"No sleeping together. Just sleep." He picked me up and put me in bed before climbing on the either side.

"Is your plan to make me so horny I'll do whatever you say? Because it's working."

"I just gave you an orgasm."

"Exactly. I've gotten two and you've had none."

He rolled me to my side facing away from him, and tucked himself to my back. "You're welcome. Go to sleep."

We lay like that for a moment, me enjoying the warmth seeping into me from his long, hard body. I pressed back into him.

"Sheriff Townsend," I purred, wiggling my rear. Your... baton...is sticking me."

"I don't have a baton."

"Oooooh, lucky me."

"Regina."

I leaned into him. "Will you just fuck me already?"

He raised himself up on an elbow, looking down on me. He was disappointed. I could tell that even in the dark.

"No," he said finally. "Go to sleep."

"I don't want to sleep. I want you to skewer me with your man meat."

Instead of laughing, he rolled to his back and groaned.

"Cole? Are you okay?"

He stood up with his pillow.

"Please, Regina, just go to sleep."

Growling, I switched on the bedside light. I was so horny I was angry. If I wasn't angry, I'd be crying, because I was in this beautiful man's bed and he still wasn't willing to sleep with me. I was that repulsive.

"What the hell is wrong with you? I swear, you have the strangest sense of honor. I am in your bed, we've been to kinky town and back, but we're not allowed to have sex? It's not like we're both virgins."

He blew out a breath. "Actually—"

"What? You are still a virgin? Oh my god, Cole." My mouth fell open and I couldn't say anything else.

He ran a hand over his head.

I found my voice. "Are you crazy? You're twenty-eight! Wait..." I felt a little shot of horror. "Are you saving yourself for marriage?"

"I was."

"Geez," I cast about for what to say. It was inconceivable to me that the hottest man I'd ever met had never done the nasty. Women all over Licking Hole would mourn if they knew. "You really took those Sunday school lessons to heart."

"It's not that. I've done other things, just not sex. But I made a decision that when I had sex, it'd be with someone special."

Of course. Cole was just the type to make a vow like that.

"So you are waiting for marriage."

"No. Just for the right one."

The right one, I realized with a pang. He was trying to tell me, nicely, I wasn't the one. It hurt more than I thought it would.

"It doesn't have to be on my wedding night," he continued. "I just want it to be right. Is that strange?"

"No, it's cool, Cole, I get it. It is so...you. You always have a plan."

He sat back down on the bed. "I didn't think it would take this long."

"You've dated before, right?"

"Yes, and I've fooled around. But I stopped when I realized I might be sending mixed messages. Then with the election, and my career—I haven't done much dating in the past few years. So it hasn't been an issue."

Except for storing up so many kinky fantasies that he blackmailed the first woman he could into carrying them out. Not that I was complaining. After my initial shock, I was actually enjoying it.

Too bad kinky degradation was all I was going to get.

"Well, whoever the lucky lady is, she's in for a treat!" I said with mock cheeriness.

"Regina—"

I cut him off. "You know, I am really tired. And we have to wake up in five hours. Time for bed, Virgin-Boy."

I flipped to my side, turned off the bedside light, and squeezed the pillow with all my might.

He said he was willing to fool around. Some perverse part of me wanted to see how far I could get him to go.

Deep down, I knew this was a game to him. A way to sow his wild oats. When it came to oat sowing, Cole Townsend was overdue. But the Cole Townsends of the world did not belong with a girl like me. I could play this game, and have some fun.

But it would never be real.

6

Five am comes really early in the morning. After burrowing under the pillows for an extra twenty minutes, Cole had to drag me out of bed. He had already shaved and showered, smelling fresh, clean and manly.

He made me make him breakfast.

"You're chipper," I muttered, watching him eat.

"I've been up a while. I went for a run."

"You were running? Why? Was a big dog chasing you?"

He didn't laugh. "I take it you don't exercise."

"I didn't get these curves from just sitting on my ass. Oh, wait, yes I did."

"Won't be doing much of that anymore." He rose to leave. "Do you have your schedule?"

"Yes. I'm oiling all the floggers today, and polishing the torture rack."

"I don't have either of those...yet. I'll be gone till late afternoon today, so behave. Or else."

A little thrill went through me. "Or else what?" I shouted after him.

"Or else I'll add a morning run to your schedule." He crooked a finger at me and I followed him to the bedroom, complaining all the way.

"Cole, I can't go running. They don't make sports bras in my size. My boobs will bounce up and hit me in the face. Probably knock me out, or give me a black eye or something."

Cole stopped at the foot of the bed. He snapped his fingers and pointed to a spot on the floor in front of him.

I went, kvetching all the way. As soon as I got close, he reached out and pulled me across his lap. Three hard slaps on my rear penetrated through my pajamas.

"That's for getting yourself off yesterday. From now on, I'm the one that gives you orgasms."

I waited until he turned his back to stick my tongue out at him. He returned with the maid costume.

"No, not that again—"

"Regina."

"Fine."

"I'm headed out now. Be good." He kissed the side of my head and a little thrill went through me, even as I stood there gritting my teeth. "If you touch yourself when I'm gone, I will get a belt for you."

"A belt?"

He pulled out his phone and showed me a picture of a metal chastity belt. The fact that he had a picture ready and waiting told me he still had a whole kinky checklist to work through.

The thought made me kinda excited.

"You better delete that before going to work. What if someone sees it?"

He chuckled. "You better worry about the pictures I have of you on my phone."

"Cole! That's blackmail," I whined, as if everything he'd done so far was above board.

"Will it work to get you to behave?

"Maybe."

He waggled a finger. "I need all the help I can get with you."

"Fine," I muttered. "It's your reputation. I've got nothing to lose."

He frowned. "What do you mean by that?"

"Exactly what I said. You're sheriff, and I'm a college dropout who just lost the only decent job she was likely to get. Stealing and selling pot are my only options."

He just shook his head.

Silly me, I didn't see the storm cloud building in his expression. I went on talking, "If you think about it, the best option for me would be turning tricks."

His face hardened into something scary. "That's not gonna happen. Regina," he snapped, when I turned away. "Get over here."

I went to him, feeling like a student called to the principal's office.

He tapped under my chin to get me to look at him. "Here's the thing, Regina. You're smart. You've always hated authority."

"No, authority always hated me. I was trailer trash, remember? I wasn't supposed to be as bright or quick as I am."

"You're right," he said after a pause. "But you always exceeded expectations. But now you're trying to live down to them. And like I said, you're above average intelligence, which means if you put your mind to it you could get into loads of trouble. You're smart enough not to get caught."

"So, you're doing this just to thwart a potential criminal mastermind?"

A hint of a smile softened his features. "That's right."

I blew out a breath. I didn't want Cole Townsend to think of me as his rehabilitation project. I wanted to be his dirty little secret. "No wonder you threatened to handcuff me to the bed."

"I want you here, where I can keep an eye on you. And I don't want your mind running in circles. I want you to stay focused on me."

No problem there, stud.

"Okay," I said, and stepped closer. Cole didn't wear cologne, but something—his body wash or soap or something—smelled fantastic. I breathed in, imagining all those muscles wet with water from the shower. Freshly washed Cole, mmm...

"Oh and Regina." His hard tone called my attention to his face. "You ever joke about prostituting yourself again, I'll spank you so hard you won't sit for days. And the minute the redness fades, I'll do it again. Not to mention keep you tied to the bed until you forget all this nonsense. Understand?"

Good grief. There went those panties. I pressed my legs together and whimpered.

"I asked you a question and I expect an answer. Do you understand?"

"Yes, sir."

"Good." He chucked me under the chin and left.

I spent the day wandering around in a vortex of lust. Chores got done, somehow, because when Cole returned, he looked around with an approving nod, and set me to dusting the giant bookshelf in his den. I actually liked handling the books—old tomes he told me he inherited from his grandfather—but Cole's proximity mixed with my raging horniness made me super bitchy. He sat on the couch, pecking at his laptop with his briefcase open beside him, and I worked around him, grumbling.

"Less talking, more cleaning," he said without lifting his eyes from the screen.

I ignored the order and continue to mutter about 'sadistic spanko sheriffs with a cleaning fetish.'

Cole left and returned, snapping his fingers to order me to him. I hated when he did that, but I didn't dare disobey.

"I have a new addition to your outfit. Open your mouth." He held up a ball gag. A wicked glint in his eyes, he popped a bright red ball into my mouth and fastened the black straps around my head. "Why didn't I think of this sooner?"

I glared at him. The ball in my mouth was large enough to keep my mouth in a perpetual 'o'. Drool collected at the corner of my mouth and he wiped it away.

"Beautiful. You are so hot right now."

My nipples hardened despite myself.

I gurgled at him.

"I can't understand you, sweetheart. But don't worry. If you're good, you get a reward." His fingers swiped at my nipples. He'd noticed I was aroused.

Bastard.

I clomped around the house in the stupid heels, moving books, and dusting and polishing surfaces carefully so as not to dirty my outfit. My only break came when he undid the gag and gave me water.

I glared as he strapped it back on and he just laughed at me and made me fetch him a beer. My face burned, but I did it, and when he snapped his fingers and pointed, I went back to cleaning his bookshelf. His eyes followed me around the room. I wasn't trying to be sexy, but bending and stooping and reaching the different level shelves gave him plenty of opportunity to view my elongated legs, my pouty ass.

I'd never been so humiliated, so objectified.

I'd also never been so turned on in my life. The edge of my skirt lifted, showing the curve of my ass as I reached high over my head to finish dusting the top shelf. Up on tiptoes, I grunted in exertion. Cole's hands came around to cup my breasts and I nearly fell over.

"Regina," Cole husked into my hair, his body molded to my back. I sank into him, breathing hard. His hands roamed up and down, from breasts to navel, and lower down, to lift my skirt and cup my mons. I groaned as two fingers pushed at my thong.

"You're wet." His voice held awe. "This turns you on?"

I nodded and widened my stance in invitation.

"Such a good girl."

His fingers dipped in and out of my pussy. I grunted from behind the gag, drool running down my cheeks. I was a mess, and I didn't care. My hips jerked in silent invitation.

"Ask before you cum," he growled as he hooked a long finger under my pubic bone, my g-spot as his target. He crooked his finger in a "cum hither" motion.

Bullseye.

I squealed. My legs shook so hard I nearly fell. My orgasm was so close...

He removed his hand, still holding me up with a strong arm under my breasts.

"Oh I forgot, you can't talk. Well, I guess you can't cum."

All manner of garbled sounds escaped from behind the

gag. His mouth dropped to my neck and my arousal soared. I begged him to fuck me.

"You may not cum." His finger brushed against my clit, and I did anyway. Cole had to hold me up as I convulsed against him, moaning behind the gag.

He turned me and I faced him, panting, my eyes wide. My orgasm had come out of nowhere and hit me like a truck. I didn't know what Cole was up to with this sexy maid, sleep in my bed but don't sleep with me business, but this game was beyond anything I'd played before. I was addicted.

"Disobeying orders already?" He looked amused by my orgasm. I didn't care if I was 'in trouble.' That climax had been worth it.

Cole stepped back, making sure I was steady on my feet. My legs felt like spaghetti, but they held me. "Hands on the wall. Ass out."

I obeyed with alacrity, and he flipped up my flimsy skirt. "Such a beautiful behind. A masterpiece." He palmed it and gave it a smack. In my mind's eye, I imagined him admiring how it jiggled. I guess it wasn't too fat for him.

"Because you came without permission, you get more punishment. Not a spanking, something more fun."

I heard him move behind me. "Bend down, stick your ass out." I jumped when Cole spread something cool between my ass cheeks.

He slipped a finger in and I cursed behind the gag.

"Relax, I'm not going to hurt you." His finger fucked me and I groaned into the wall. It didn't hurt, but it didn't feel good. I didn't know what to think about the sensation, but the humiliation was making me drip.

"See this?" He showed me a metal bulb with a red jewel on the end. "This is going in your ass."

I protested and he ordered me to face the wall again. One hand clamped on the back of my neck, holding me still while the other slid the plug between my cheeks.

"I'm gonna train your ass for me," he rasped. This must be turning him on as much as it did me. "You're gonna walk around my house plugged and ready. I own your ass now. Whenever I snap my fingers, you're going to bend over and show me what I own."

I felt something poke my bunghole. Hard and unyielding, the plug stretched me open a little. Fuck.

I moaned as he twisted it in. "It the smallest I have. Complain and I'll go up a size."

My head thunked against the wall.

"Oh, I forgot." He chuckled. "You can't complain. You're gagged."

For a few minutes, he played with my bottom, squeezing each cheek, lifting and parting them. I almost got used to the foreign object filling me, but he pulled me away from the wall and the movement made the plug feel strange all over again.

He kissed my forehead. "You're doing so well. Go to the kitchen and make me a sandwich."

In the kitchen, I spread mustard on bread, tingling with arousal. The plug made me feel full and very, very aware of the sensations between my legs.

As I walked back to the den, plate in hand and body trembling so much I had to focus on putting one foot in front of the other, I realized I hadn't worried about anything all day. Not my mom, not my bills. I set Cole's lunch down in front of him and waited for my next order. I still struggled with my thoughts—the casual degradation filled me with anger and arousal. I loved and hated what he did to me, but I couldn't deny that he'd kept his promise.

This brilliant and beautiful sadist had given me peace.

From the tent at the front of his trousers, he wasn't entirely unaffected.

"Regina," Cole's voice broke into my thoughts, and I went to him. He'd eaten his sandwich and set it aside on the couch, and now he wanted dessert.

I came to stand between his legs and he unbuckled the gag. As I worked the kinks out of my jaw, his hands roved up and down my body.

"I love how you look at me," he groaned. "Like I'm superman. Like I can do no wrong."

I arched my back, pushing my breasts into his hands. "You can't. I do all the wrong things for you."

"Not anymore."

Growing bolder, I leaned over him. My hand snaked over his abs and ventured lower. "I like being naughty."

He sucked in a breath.

It was now or never. I had planned on seducing Cole, I just didn't realize it would happen this fast. He wouldn't sleep with me? Fine. There were other things we could do.

"I want your cock," I purred.

"Regina—"

"It's okay, Cole." I dropped to my knees. "It's what we both want. Let me please you."

I waited until he nodded before I undid his pants and took him out. He was long and thick and my pussy clenched at the sight.

One day, Cole would meet his special lady. In my head, she was blonde and thin and perfect—everything I was not. "Fuck you, sister," I thought. Cole could wait for her all he wanted, but right now he was mine, and after all the kinky shit I'd done, I'd earned a reward.

Taking a deep breath, I sucked him down.

I used every trick I knew, licking as I bobbed my head. Above me, Cole's great body tensed. His head fell back and fingers gripped the couch cushions.

He gasped my name as he came and I swallowed.

"That was..."

"Just part of my duties. Shall I add cock service to the regular schedule, sir?"

Cole didn't answer. Instead, his long finger teased down the neckline of my maid's outfit. I let him pull it down, jutting out my breasts as he played with my nipples. I never thought I'd be so happy on my knees, topless with a plug in my ass, but my drippy pussy had no complaints. One touch to my clit and I would explode.

I sighed when he pulled my top up. "Back to work. I have things to do."

"Whatever you say, sir." I smirked. I was hoping he'd order me to the bedroom, but the week was still young. I felt his eyes follow me out of the room.

7

Two days passed, and despite my best efforts, Cole never again lost control. Oh, sure, he had me kneel and suck him off, almost every day. Sometimes he got me off, sometimes he didn't. But it didn't get me any closer to what I really wanted.

Every day I came within inches of breaking down and begging, 'Please just have sex with me!' Days became endless agony. For every sexual torment or humiliation Cole put me through, I imagined a thousand more. Each time he put his hands between my legs, I was a sopping mess.

The nights were ten times worse. If I went to bed without him, I'd lay awake listening for him to come home, open the fridge and eat whatever I'd left for him, then come into the bedroom. My heart always beat faster—maybe this would be the night! But no. And it turns out sleeping with your dream man without being able to actually *sleep* with him means little rest. For both of us.

One night, I tossed and turned but couldn't get to sleep. Cole threw a heavy leg over mine to keep me still. I thought he would sleep then, but he lay awake with me, stroking my chest under the nightshirt.

"Please stop," I said and his hand stilled.

"You don't like it?"

"No, I do. Too much. Never mind, keep going. And if you want to warm up your dick, feel free to climb on. I'm clean, and on birth control. You don't even need a condom."

His deep sigh stirred my hair. I pressed my lips together against anger, or tears, or both. If Cole didn't want me, why was he keeping me around? I wasn't his dream woman, but did I have to be her placeholder, only fit to warm her side of the bed?

"Why don't you just make me sleep somewhere else?"

He pushed his face into my hair. I didn't want him to speak, to break the spell. But I had to know.

"I used to lie awake thinking about you. I worried all the time."

I pressed my body back against him and he groaned.

"You have no idea how good it feels to have you here. In my bed, I know you're safe from almost everything."

I wondered what he meant by 'almost everything.' "Of course I'm safe. I'm always safe when I'm with you."

He remained quiet so long I thought he'd fallen asleep. But right before my own sleep took me, I heard him whisper, "I hope so."

AFTER A FEW DAYS living with Cole, it made sense why he never had a steady girlfriend. His work schedule would try the most understanding woman's patience. Not mine, though. I didn't feel that I deserved his attention in the first place. I genuinely began to think of how I could make his life easier. Not that I'd ever admit it. I took every opportunity to annoy the hell out of him. I seemed to have the knack.

One day, I walked into the kitchen and found his gun, badge and handcuffs on the table. Cole was in the other room on the phone. I'd never held a gun before, and there it lay on the table, black and dangerous. My fingers itched to touch the forbidden. Had Cole ever had to use it?

I knew there was a dark side to Licking Hole. I'd flirted with it, literally—I'd dated a boy who worked in his father's shady business. Donnie DeMarco bragged about it to me as if it was funny, but when I met his father, I felt the undercurrent of violence. Donnie's father was nice to me, but was full of hate for the people he chose to cheat. He talked about society like it was a club he couldn't join. Us and them.

I dumped Donnie so I didn't have to watch his father teach him that hate.

When I started embezzling, I wondered how much he had taught me. Was my past a black hole, just waiting to suck me in?

I reached for the gun, diverting at the last second to pick up the handcuffs. Like so many other kids I grew up with, I'd come close to wearing these for real. Only Cole kept that from happening.

A hand wrapped around my throat from behind. Cole's body pressed against my back, hard and dominating. I dropped the handcuffs with a clatter.

"Gah! How are you so quiet?"

The heat at my back, and hand at my neck made me still. Cole's breath hit my ear.

"What are you doing, Regina?"

"Tidying up."

"Do I really have to tell you not to touch my gear?"

"It's not my fault you leave your stuff lying around

everywhere."

I swallowed hard. My pulse beat against his palm.

"You were thinking about touching my gun, weren't you?"

"Yes," I said, breathless. "You know me. I'm always ready to touch your...gun."

He laughed softly. "Naughty girl. What am I going to do with you?"

"If I can make a suggestion—"

"No." He stepped back, grabbed my wrist, and pulled me into the living room.

"Kneel," he ordered. I did, looking up at him.

He cuffed one of my arms to the coffee table. I'd set a laundry basket full of clean clothes to be folded on the coach, and he dumped these onto my lap.

"Here. You wanted to touch my stuff."

He sat on the couch and I folded laundry at his feet. It was a bitch with one of my hands secured, and I complained about it until he ordered me to shut up. I did, for a few seconds.

"Have you ever fired your gun?"

He raised a brow at me from behind the papers he was reading. "I plead the fifth."

I rolled my eyes.

"I'm a cop. Of course I've fired a gun."

"But I mean, have you fired that one? At someone?" He looked at me with a face of stone, and I felt a chill. "Oh my god, you have, haven't you?"

He kept reading his papers, and I fell silent. I didn't want to know. I wracked my brain for a way to change the mood.

"What about a car chase? Have you done many of those?"

"This is Licking Hole, not the Dukes of Hazzard."

"Not even for a beer run at half time?" I joked, and got a stern look from over his laptop screen.

"Power is wasted on you responsible types," I muttered, angling my body to fold one of Cole's t-shirts.

"I'm going to pretend I didn't hear that."

"If I was a cop, I'd speed everywhere. Pretend I was chasing people."

"If you were a cop, society would be doomed."

"Hey! I'd be amazing."

"You just told me how you'd abuse your power."

"I can be responsible when I put my mind to it."

He raised a brow

"Okay, not really. But I'm learning."

"Yes, you are. And that, my dear, is why you are hand-cuffed to the coffee table, folding my laundry at my feet." He leaned down to kiss me. I let him. I wanted to comment on how turned on I got by humiliation, but had a feeling he already knew.

Just sitting at his feet made me wet.

"What is the point of folding clothes? You're just going to wear them the next day."

In answer he got up, left the room, and returned with the ball gag.

"Open." He fixed the straps around my head while I tried to kill him with my eyes.

"I hate you, you bastard," I said. With the gag it came out "uh huh huh, huh huh huh."

"Be polite." He wagged a finger in my face.

"Urr."

∼

"WE NEED TO TALK."

I finished clearing away his breakfast and danced over with a coffee refill. I'd gotten pretty graceful on the high, high heels.

Cole motioned me to sit.

"It's been a week, and I'd like to talk about what happens next."

A week of humiliations and perpetual horniness. I got my fair share of orgasms, and so did Cole, but I hadn't gotten him inside me in the way it really counted. I wasn't looking for a declaration of love. Or maybe I was. But I'd settle for a declaration of lust.

"Regina, are you listening to me?"

"What? Yes! Just say the last thing you just said again."

"I told you Monday you start volunteering."

"Where?"

"I haven't decided. But you don't need to know. You just need to be ready."

"Fine. You sure I just couldn't be your secretary? I'll wear stockings and garters and kitten heel pumps. And blow you under the desk."

"No." He shook his head. He proffered his coffee cup. I sighed and filled it, ignoring how serving him made my pussy clench.

"Oh, why not?" I pouted as I finished pouring.

"Conflict of interest," he grunted. "People think we're living together. I can't pull strings to hire you."

"As if there isn't enough nepotism going on around here." I grouched. "I'd be so good, too." I put a hand to my ear pretending it was a phone. "Welcome to Licking Bottom, how can I help you?"

Cole spat coffee into his newspaper. I watched in delight as he sputtered. "Regina, what the hell?"

I made sure I was out of arm's reach but couldn't stop my

grin.

"Very funny," Cole said through clenched teeth, dabbing a napkin at his wet suit. He rose and went off to change. As he passed me, he smacked my ass so hard I jumped.

"You love it!" I called after him.

I was on hands and knees, wiping the mess off the floor when two polished shoes stopped in front of me.

"I'm off to the meeting," he said, and hesitated.

"What?" I rose up to tall knees. He looked so handsome in his uniform. The last sheriff had opted to wear a suit most of the time, emphasizing the time he spent in meetings versus patrolling like a regular cop. No matter how busy he got, Cole took a shift on the regular beat every week. Just his way of keeping his finger on the pulse of the community, he told me. The night he'd caught me he'd been on patrol.

"I'll be back pretty late. I may not have time to get you to your mom's."

His truck sat in the driveway and the keys were hanging by the door, but I didn't mention that. He probably wasn't ready to trust me driving his vehicle. Smart man.

"Do you think you can wait until tomorrow morning to see your mom?"

I checked in with my gut, and the biggest feeling was relief. "I think so."

Cole studied me. I had the feeling he'd known I'd be glad to skip a visit.

"You're a good daughter," he said.

I scrambled to my feet, mumbling something about getting the laundry. Cole caught my arm, halting me mid-escape.

"I mean it. You've done the best you can. No mother could ask for more."

I sucked in a breath, praying my tears wouldn't fall.

Turning my back to Cole, I said, "I don't know about that. I could make a bunch of money and buy her a house. Or at least send her on a cruise."

Cole wrapped his arms around me. I fixed my eyes forward. If I looked back at him, I'd burst into tears.

"All's I need is a few grand," I added.

"Oh yeah? How are you going to earn that?

"I once dated a guy whose dad owned a chop shop. I bet I could get some money off parts of your truck."

He spun me around. "Are you seriously joking about that?"

I giggled.

"Young lady, you're gonna regret that."

I grinned at his furious expression. "You're going to be late."

Glancing at the clock, he bit back a curse.

"Wait here."

He stomped off, and I heard him on his cell, explaining he was running behind schedule. When he returned to the kitchen, he still looked pissed.

Excellent.

With a snap of his fingers, he ordered me to stand in front of him. "I'll be back tonight, but even if I'm not, you're going to behave."

"Always, sir." I fluttered my lashes.

"Just to make sure..." He fixed the ball gag around my head. Then he cuffed my hands behind my back.

"Ut uh 'ell?" I screamed as best I could through the gag.

"This should keep you busy and out of trouble."

I glowered even as he kissed my head.

"I'll bring sandwiches for dinner. Oh, and Regina," he called halfway to the door.

"Oooh?"

"Don't forget the laundry."

AFTER A HALF HOUR of handcuff hell, I glanced out the window and realized Cole hadn't left. He sat in his patrol car, a cell phone at his ear. I stood and made sad puppy eyes at him until he glanced up. He sighed and exited the car. The first thing he did when he returned was undo the gag and the handcuffs. I massaged my jaw as he chafed my wrists.

"Did you learn your lesson?"

"Yes." I resisted the urge to roll my eyes. As much as I liked goading Cole, I didn't want a repeat of the past half hour. "You didn't leave?" A part of me guessed he wouldn't leave me so helpless.

"I'm going to go now. I wanted you to know that tomorrow you start volunteering."

"You chose a place?"

"Nope. Mr. Roberts did."

My gut clenched like I'd been kicked. "Is he...is he very angry with me?"

"Not gonna lie, Regina. When he first found out you took the money, he was hurt. Not angry, though. He cares about you, almost like a daughter."

I knew that. Before I went to college, I'd given him a thank you card with my high school picture in it. He kept the picture on the shelf with framed photos of his whole family.

"If you'd only stolen from him once, and told him right away, he probably wouldn't have fired you."

"I really fucked up didn't I?" Tears filled my eyes. "I'm such a screw up. Total waste of space." My voice sounded defeated and pathetic, even to my ears. "I wish my mother had just gotten an abortion. Everyone would be better off."

Cole moved so fast I didn't see him until I was over his lap receiving the first hard swat. He kept spanking, harsher and harsher until I was wriggling and crying.

Just as quickly, it was over. Cole set me on my feet and fixed me with the sternest stare I'd yet to see. "Regina. If I ever hear you say that again, or talking down, you will think that spanking was a walk in the park. Understand?"

I bobbed my head up and down. Anything to avoid that punishing palm. My hand crept back to rub my bottom, and Cole caught it in his firm grip.

"Answer me."

"I understand."

"Good girl." His tone softened, and he pulled me into his lap. I lay tucked against him on my side and he rubbed my bottom until I relaxed against him. I stayed very quiet. The spanking had undone me, but it had also stemmed the tide of self-disgust. No one had ever cared enough about me to stop me talking down on myself. Cole's violent reaction both shocked and steadied me.

"Feeling better?"

"Yes. Sorry."

"It's okay, sweetheart." Cole kissed my shoulder. "I told you I'd take care of you, and I will. But I won't tolerate anyone saying bad things about you. Not even you.

"Thank you," I said, and meant it.

He chucked me under the chin. "I've got to get back to work. I'm going to be pretty busy for a few days, but I'll make sure you're occupied. The minute I get a chance, we're going to resolve the situation with Mr. Roberts, once and for all."

"Okay," I said, though I didn't like the sound of that.

8

The days settled into a routine, with Cole working long hours, as he'd warned me. I wondered if he kept himself busy so he could keep his hands off me longer. It pleased me to think I was that much of a temptation. Of course, the more he stayed away, the more I wanted him. Whenever he worked from home, I made myself as loud and obnoxious as I could, which only earned me the gag. Often I found myself watching him, admiring the grace in his long fingers on the keyboard, the timber of his voice as he gave someone instructions.

"Regina," he called one day, without looking up from his papers. "You're doing it again."

I blinked. "Sorry."

"Keep it up and I'll give you a new rule—no looking above crotch level."

"That's only going to make it worse." I went back to my work, only to look up when a shadow fell over my hands.

Cole stood behind me, tracing the delicate strap of my skimpy outfit. His touch spread tingles through me.

I turned to face him. We were mere inches apart. "Cole?"

"Regina," he said, and then he was all over me. Touching, kissing, claiming, his hands sliding up and down my body as I pressed myself into him and whimpered. When the kiss ended and we broke apart, both of us were breathless.

"Bedroom," he ordered. "It's time."

Squee!

But when I got there, I saw a wooden rectangle on the bed, and realized what he meant. Cole stalked into the bedroom after me. I met his eyes, once, and saw darkness there. I didn't look at his face again.

"Strip."

Slowly, I removed the little white apron. "What's going to happen?"

"I told you you'd get paddled for stealing. I think you need it."

I let the maid outfit fall to the floor. "Will it hurt?"

"Yes."

I stood to the side of the bed, arms wrapped around myself watching Cole remove his shirt and belt. His bare chest was a thing of beauty, a product of his daily run and five hundred pushups executed in crisp, military style.

He motioned for me to move to the foot of the bed. My breathing picked up as he picked up the paddle and examined it, before setting it down and picking up his belt. He doubled it over and tested it against his palm, snapping it. I jumped.

Cole crooked a finger at me to get me to come closer. Close to hyperventilating, I obeyed. The man couldn't be more intimidating with an executioner's hood.

His fingers curled around my hips, warm and reassuring. "It'll hurt, but it'll feel good."

I let out a broken laugh. "How's that?"

"After this punishment, it's over. You're forgiven. We never have to speak of it again."

He waited for me to answer, but for once in my life, I couldn't speak. I'd do anything for this man, but he never stopped pushing the boundaries of where I wanted to go.

After a minute of silence, he laid the belt on the bed. "Regina, look at me."

I did, and he rewarded me by cradling my face in his hands. His hazel eyes, his aquiline nose, his handsome features blurred.

"We don't have to do this," he said.

"Yes, we do." Somehow not going through with this discipline was worse. Not only did I deserve it, but worse, I'd let down Cole.

"Do you trust me?"

"Yes."

"Then get into position."

I put my hands on the bed, stuck my bottom out as the target.

Cole ran a finger down.

"Hand first, then belt, then paddle."

His hand clamped on the back of my neck and I steeled myself.

The blow didn't come. Instead, his long fingers danced between my legs, strumming my clit to a fever pitch. I gasped, and writhed, teetering on the edge of orgasm.

"Being turned on will make this less painful," he said. "I told you, Regina, I'm going to take care of you."

At his words, I relaxed completely. His left hand remained at my neck as his right squeezed my bottom. He didn't have to hold me down, but his touch made me relax. I could struggle all I wanted; he wouldn't let me get away.

Cole started spanking me. Light at first, then building at

a steady crescendo. He paid particular attention to my sit spots, but even my thighs got a few swats. After a few minutes, the swats grew harder. I ground my chest into the bed, gritting my teeth. I didn't cry out, though. The slow buildup meant I could take the pain.

My bottom stung and felt red hot to touch by the time Cole finished the hand spanking. I wasn't anywhere near my limit. He stopped and palmed my bottom, squeezing and releasing. The rough massage worked the sting away.

"You okay?"

"Yes," my reply came muffled by the bed.

I heard him moving behind me and braced myself. Up next was the belt.

The first lash sliced across my bottom and I reared up off the bed.

"Back in position."

"I'm sorry," I gasped.

"Do you want me to hold you down?" Without waiting for an answer, he put a hand between my shoulder blades and pushed me back down onto the bed.

The next blows with the belt made me jump, but I realized I could breathe through the pain. It burned and then faded.

"You'll think twice before breaking the law again. You pull anything like that again, you'll answer to me."

I gasped as he laid a lash over a previous one. My hands flew back to protect my bottom, and he quickly captured them and held them in the small of my back. The next few lashes came down harder, and I realized how much he'd been holding back.

"Ow," I cried. "I'm sorry."

"You're gonna be." The belt caught my lower buttocks, blazing a trail across my sit spots.

I cursed.

"Do you need me to gag you? Swear again and I'll get soap."

"No." Somehow I knew being unable to call out would make things worse. "Please. I'll be good."

"You better be. From now on, you get so much as a speeding ticket, you answer to me." The belt came down again and again. "And if you find yourself in trouble, you ask for help. No more riding it out alone."

I didn't ask him to stop. The pain seared through me, cleansing fire. I cried out the tears I'd bottled up for years, ever since a phone call about my mother's condition dragged me out of my sophomore year, back home. It wasn't fair.

"What's not fair?" Cole asked, and I realized I'd spoken out loud.

"My life! Everything!"

"Talk to me, Regina." He dropped the belt on the bed, and massaged my bottom.

"I'd gotten out! I'd almost escaped this hell hole. I survived my childhood here. Wasn't that enough?"

"That's it, let it out."

"I hate this place! I hate my life! I just want to leave."

He sat and pulled me into his arms. "When you came back to take care of your mom, you didn't ask for help. Why?"

"I didn't think anyone would—"

"Your old boss gave you your job back without a second thought."

"I didn't want to ask for anything more than that. I didn't deserve it."

He tugged me closer. His hand rested at the back of my neck, holding me against him.

"You deserve it."

He ended the hug and I almost cried out at the loss of his arms around my body.

"Almost done. Back into position." His tone was incredibly gentle.

I moved, resting my head on one arm. I reached for his hand with the other. He took it.

I squeezed his fingers as he tapped the paddle against my bottom.

"This will hurt," he warned.

The blow took the breath from my lungs. But then I was falling, floating softly into another place. I relaxed, gave in, and let Cole take over.

A few more sharp taps with the paddle, but the pain felt far, far away.

"One more." It cracked down a final time, and felt as if Cole had hit me with all his might. I cried out.

It was over.

Tears leaked out of my eyes.

"Shh, Regina. Forever. You're forgiven." Cole rocked me in his arms until the storm passed, my big, gulping sobs quieted.

"Cole, I—" I started to say *I love you*. But that wasn't what I meant. Whatever I felt went deeper than love. *I love you, I've always loved you, I'll love you forever*, was more like it. But I couldn't say that without knowing he was ready to hear it. He'd asked me to obey him, and I had. He'd said nothing about love. "Thank you."

He lifted me and put me to bed. As soon as he lay down behind me, his arm wrapped around me and pulled my body flush to his.

I lay there quietly, filled with the floaty feeling. Eventually, though, I came down. Thoughts raced through my head in time to my throbbing bottom.

"Cole? What are we doing? Do you know?"

He seemed to understand what I was asking. "I'm claiming you."

"Claiming me? Like what, I Tarzan you Jane sort of thing? Isn't that sort of old fashioned?"

"I guess I'm old fashioned then."

"I'll say."

"Regina." His voice, like his touch, was firm and soothing at the same time. "Stop fighting this."

"I have to fight," I whispered. "If I don't fight...I'll give in completely."

"That's it, baby. That's what I want." He pulled me closer, into his arms. His lips found my ear. "Give in to me."

"You don't understand. I'm afraid I won't be able to stop. Cole," I pushed away from his chest to meet his eyes. "You've always been my weak spot."

Excitement flared in his eyes. "Then let go and give us what we both want."

"I'm scared."

"Baby. You can trust me. You know that."

I nodded, and let him hug me again. I'd never felt anything so good as Cole's arms around me, his firm chest under my cheek.

"I'm going to take care of you," he said. "You know I will."

"I do. I just don't know why you'd want to."

"Because you're mine." His hands slid up and down my back, setting every nerve afire. "You were always mine."

9

Cole's phone rang, breaking the spell between us.

He groaned. "I have to take this."

I rolled out of bed as soon as he left the room, and went to the mirror. My ass was as red as expected, but not bruised...yet. All in all, it wasn't as bad as I thought.

You were always mine.

Cole's words echoed through my head. Did they mean what I thought they did? Or was he just stating the obvious? Of course I belonged to him. But was he mine?

The answer to that question would either break me, or set me up for life. Either way, fear gripped me.

Miserable, I crawled back into bed. I was so in love with him I couldn't breathe. It overwhelmed me. This whole week I'd done everything on his stupid list. I scrubbed the man's toilet for godssake, and felt blissfully happy. If that wasn't love, I don't know what is.

Did he reciprocate? Was all this business of "claiming me" teasing? Just a game to him? He had everything handed to him on a platter. Worse, he didn't take it for granted. He worked hard. He was the finest, most upstanding citizen of Licking Hole, maybe even the entire state.

And I belonged in jail.

Cole's voice echoed down the hall and I settled back on my side of the bed.

It wouldn't work. The sheriff and the screw up. The golden boy and the girl from the wrong side of the tracks.

Cole finished his call and returned to the bedroom. "Regina?"

I didn't answer. I lay on my side with my eyes squeezed shut, pretending to sleep.

After a moment, he lay down and fell asleep beside me. I let my breath out then, a quiet whine against the hurt I felt in my chest. Lying next to a man, knowing he could never love me—the pain of the punishment had nothing on this.

I WAS quiet the morning he drove me to volunteer. No more protesting. I had to finish up my time with Cole, and get the hell out. He'd tire of me and let me go. I just had to be a good little Regina, and obey without complaint.

My silent vow lasted until Cole pulled up to a pretty brick building with sign reading "Maple Grove Senior Assisted Living."

"No," I said. "This is where you want me to volunteer? No way."

"You promised."

"I can't."

"Just try. For me. Just do as I say. Don't think about anything else."

Silently, I cussed him out.

A well-dressed woman with short, curly hair stood on the curb waiting for me.

"I'm Betty," she said, shaking my hand. She looked about as old as my mother, and though she had a no-nonsense handshake, she wore a big smile. "I'm the activities director here at Maple Grove."

Activities director?

She waved goodbye to Cole and turned to me, cocking her head. "Sheriff Townsend says you're between jobs and volunteering until you find a new career?"

I shrugged. "Something like that."

"We'll go easy on you. You're going to be helping me in the Orchard."

"The Orchard?"

"What we call the wing of our facility that houses our dementia patients. Right this way."

I took a moment to mentally murder Cole before I followed.

The door opened to the dreaded scene. But instead of the horror show I expected, I saw a pretty room with cream wallpaper. There were even a few potted plants. Residents in wheelchairs faced a TV, but some also sat at tables playing with a craft.

Everything seemed neat and clean, and while not all of the residents were smiling, it looked like they had a good life. Maybe even better than mom's in the trailer.

I waited to reserve judgment until after Betty's tour. She showed me everything, from the kitchen to the residents' rooms. She ran the residents' social calendar, and took fun seriously.

"Thursdays Jenny White comes from Licking Hole Fitness and leads the residents in aerobics. Well, she plays music and gets them to move as much as they can. It seems to be good for morale. And Friday we always have a party."

"What about today?"

"I hoped you might have some ideas," Betty said. "Why don't you get out among the residents, see what they'd like?"

By lunchtime—served at 11 am—I mingled with the residents.

"You're so pretty. Are you married?" a white-haired lady asked.

"Uh, no."

"But you're so pretty!"

I saw Betty wave me over, pointing excitedly to a box of supplies. "Uh, thank you. I think I have to go—"

"Of course. Go cook dinner for your husband."

"Oh, no, I'm not married."

"But you're so pretty!"

And so on.

My big breakthrough came when one of the ladies, a Mrs. Jameson, challenged me to a game of canasta. I organized a group of six, but I didn't know the rules, and she didn't remember them. In the end, we made them up.

"Hearts!" one gentleman shouted, and we all laid down our cards, groaning.

Betty walked by, nodding approval. On my suggestion, she'd gotten another group of octogenarian residents around the table, coloring like kindergarteners.

By the end of the day, I had a list of ideas for her, including casino night and more senior aerobics. Several gentlemen requested the return of Jenny White the fitness lady. She was good for their moral. Or, at least, her tight, spandex clad ass was.

I didn't realize how many hours had passed until Mrs. Jameson started clapping in excitement. Cole stood in the doorway, casual in jeans and a t-shirt. My heart skipped a beat.

"What a handsome man! Is that your husband?"

"No, ma'am. But he is my ride."

She nodded knowingly. "You better go home and cook him dinner. You don't want that one to get away."

"Did you have a good day?" Cole asked as I ran up to him. I nodded and blushed as one of the residents shouted, "kiss him!" and let out a wolf whistle. I grabbed his hand and pulled him outside before Cole got any ideas. A visit from the local sheriff was another idea for Betty's Calendar of Fun. Cole would be a big hit with the residents. If all else failed, I could just make out with him in front of everyone.

"What are you smiling about?"

"Nothing." I smoothed my features.

"I guess you had a good day."

"It was all right." I let my thoughts wander, and Cole let me. We got home, and I put on my costume without him asking, and made dinner.

After the meal, he set down his fork and caught my hand.

"What's on your mind, Regina? It's not like you to be so quiet."

"Maple Grove...how much does a place like that cost?"

"A lot of money."

I sagged in my seat. "Figured."

"Don't tell anyone this, but I heard that some employees get pretty substantial discounts."

I glanced over at him sharply. It sounded too good to be true. "There aren't any positions open. Betty told me that."

"Yes, but Betty wants to retire."

I went still. It sounded too good to be true.

"Do you think if I volunteered there for a few months, I'd be a good candidate for the job?"

"I think you'd be a shoo-in."

I closed my eyes. I wanted this so badly for my mom I couldn't breathe.

"It won't work. I need money, now."

"My guess is that Betty might hire on someone part time sooner rather than later. As for the rest...it just so happens I need a live in maid for the next few months. It pays pretty well."

I smiled. "Does it now? I hear it's worth it just for the other...perks."

"Is that what we're calling orgasms now?"

"If you like." My smile fell away. "I can't ask you to pay me."

"You didn't ask. I offered. What's more, I'll pay your bills directly, and order you to accept it." He rose and cleared his dishes and mine. I stared at the woodgrain on the table, wondering if things could really get better, wondering if I dared to hope.

"If your mom moves there, you could sell the trailer. Move in permanently. Maybe even go back to college, finish up your degree. They have a commuter program. I checked."

I closed my eyes. "Cole, I can't."

"Course you can. I'd pay for it."

My eyes flew open. The handsome man across from me offered a smile that looked almost shy. And I realized that for the past few days, I'd been living in a dream.

Time to wake up.

"Why?" I asked. I made my voice hard.

"Why?" He frowned. I noticed his cheeks were flushed.

"You heard me, Cole." I leaned forward. "Why would

you do this? Why wouldn't you just arrest me that night? Anyone else would've gotten in trouble."

"Haven't we been over this?"

"No. You never really answered. You say things like *I'm claiming you* and *you're mine* and I just go with it. But I don't know what any of it means."

"Isn't it obvious?" Now his neck was just as flushed as his face.

"No." I suddenly was fighting tears. If it wasn't important enough for him to say how he felt about me, then all of this was blackmail. And I was no better than a whore.

"Because I like you, Regina."

Fury surged through me. "Like?" I waved my hand at the kitchen. "I am wearing a ridiculous costume. I even wore these torture things for you-" Reaching down, I pulled off the shoes and threw them at his head.

Cole raised his arms and pushed back in his chair. He started to rise and I beat him to it, standing so fast my own chair almost fell over.

"And all's you can say is that you like me?" I screeched so loud the neighbors could hear.

"Regina, look." His cheeks burned red as if I'd slapped him. I didn't know if he was angry or embarrassed. "I'm not good with words like you—"

"Try, Cole."

He took a deep breath and—

Nothing.

I shoved my chair back and stomped to the living room.

"I've got to go."

Cole followed. "What are you doing?"

"What I should have done in the first place, instead of embezzling. Find some rich guy and suck his dick until he pays all my bills. Someone who isn't you. All this time I should've used my body and I've been trying to use my brain. Silly me. Thanks for enlightening me."

I picked up his landline—he kept one as sheriff. He took the phone out of my hand and threw it against the wall, where it shattered.

"What do you think this is?" He advanced. "You think this is some sort of game? That I would tell you I'm claiming you and then sit back and watch you walk out to another guy?"

I backed away. "Cole, I—"

"Answer me," he shouted.

"You're scaring me."

He gripped my chin. He still looked pissed but his touch was gentle. "Good. Maybe then you'll understand."

"Understand what?" I pushed his hand away. "You make me do all these things for me, and you can't even say what I am to you? A lover...a friend...a hot piece of ass? Just tell me where I stand!"

Cole's chest rose and fell like he'd just run a mile. "I can't."

"Why not? Isn't it enough that I obey you? That I want to be with you? I know you're waiting for someone special—I just want it to be me!"

"Don't you get it? It is you."

"What?" I dropped to the couch like my legs had been cut out from under me.

"It's always been you."

"Then why—"

"I had to be sure." He rubbed his hand over his head. "I wanted you to be sure. I don't just want sex with you, Regina. I want it all."

I shook my head, not understanding.

"I want this." He waved his hand at my outfit. "I like

spanking you. And controlling you. And overpowering you. I'm not normal, Regina. I never have been. I look at you, this beautiful woman, and I want to control you. I don't want to settle down and treat you like a queen. I mean, I do, but here, and in the bedroom, I want to spank your ass raw and have you serve me on your knees. And I want to do more. I like having you as my slave. I need it."

I studied his tense face. "Is that it?"

"I needed to know you could handle it."

"Let me get this straight." I stood up, but I was shorter than him. Climbing on the couch, I looked him in the eye. Standing on the furniture was probably against the rules, but Cole didn't comment. "You've wanted me all this time. You just wanted to be sure I was sure."

"Yes."

"All of this has been a test?"

"I have these urges," he said. "You need to understand what I am."

"What are you, Cole?"

He pressed his lips together.

"You're not a freak," I reassured him. "You're a dominant. You like control. Guess what, Cole?" I indicated my outfit. "I'm okay with it."

"I have this darkness inside me..."

I cupped the side of his face. "I love your darkness."

He leaned into my palm, his eyes fluttering closed. His long lashes lay against his fine, flawless skin. His beauty was so unreal, it amazed me that I could touch it.

I bent my head to his. "Let me be your dream girl," I whispered. "I'll do whatever you want. I want to be your fantasy."

Please, please, let it be me, I pleaded silently. I held my breath like a prayer as his hand came up and clasped the back of my neck. His touch remained gentle, but he tightened his fingers slightly to hold my forehead against his.

"I can't stand the thought of anyone else touching you," he said. "I know I'm crazy but...I'm crazy about you. If I take you, I'm never letting you go." He opened his eyes. The honesty there hit me like a blow. "You agree to be with me, and then get mad and try to leave, I'll hunt you down. If anyone tried to take you from me, I'll hurt him. Does that scare you?"

"No." Wrapping my hand around his neck, I took a deep breath, and told the truth. "Cole, I've always belonged to you. Always."

He kissed me, and then his hands were everywhere, touching me, claiming me. His hands went under my bottom, lifting me from the couch and setting me down to my feet. His kisses were ferocious, and I gave as good as I got.

He pulled at my top and I heard it tear. I struggled out of it, ripping it further. We kissed like we were dying, and the touch of the other's lips held the cure.

I pulled away for a second. "Smack my ass."

"Regina," he groaned.

"Fucking do it," I said, and winced a second later when his palm connected with my ass. Pain reverberated through me, bringing my body to life. "Harder."

He sat and pulled me across his lap. His left hand clamped down on the back of my neck, holding me down as he spanked me harder.

"Like that?" He thrust two fingers into my sopping pussy, finger fucking me roughly. It would've hurt if I wasn't so wet.

"Yes," I moaned.

He pulled his fingers out and gave me a vicious swat. "You're going to be my naughty girl."

"Always. You better fucking keep me in line."

"Language." He slapped the top of my thigh. "You better mind. Or you're going to get a lot worse than my hand."

I reared off his knees, fighting as much as I could. "Prove it."

He pushed me to the floor. I ended up sprawled at his feet, cheek to carpet, ass in the air. I heard the snap of leather a second before he struck me with his belt. I cried out, and he stopped.

Bracing my hands against the carpet, I pushed my ass up higher and demanded, "More."

The belt bit down. Pain sliced through me. Again, and again.

I shook with desire.

"You're going to learn," Cole emphasized his words with another strike.

Quivering on the floor, I couldn't answer. Arousal flooded through me until all I could think of was Cole taking me, claiming me. Each lick of the belt was a kiss—hard and dominating. I could take the pain. I could take anything from him.

By the time he threw down the belt and knelt beside me, the pain felt miles away.

"You okay?" He pushed my hair out of my face.

I nodded as much as I could with my head down, and ass up in the air.

He drew my head back with a fist in my hair. "You trust me."

My eyes watered with the sting, and I blinked them away. "Always."

He let go and I sagged back to my hands and knees.

"To the bedroom, sweetheart. Crawl."

I crawled. By the time we got to the bedroom, I didn't dare stop, lest I leave a puddle on the floor.

"You're doing so well," he told me as he pulled me up by my hair and guided me into position. My front half lay on the bed; my bottom poked back at him, a perfect target.

I steeled myself for the lash.

It never came.

Stubbled cheeks scraped my tender backside, making me cry out. Cole's tongue probed into the crevice, and I cried out for a different reason.

Lurching forward, I tried to scramble onto the bed, but Cole held my thighs in an iron grip, pulling me back against his mouth. He'd dropped to his knees behind me as he ate me out. I gave up fighting and panted against the bedspread.

Between the soreness in my bottom and the hot mouth on my mons, I was beyond ecstasy. The pain made each lick of pleasure ten times more powerful.

I screamed my orgasm into the sheets. He flipped me onto my back, holding my wrists over my head as he loomed over me.

I felt him at my entrance. My eyes widened.

"Are you sure?"

"Regina, it was you. Always."

Releasing one of my wrists, he guided himself inside me and cursed.

"Cole Townsend, did you just cuss?"

"Yes." He held himself still, sweat beading on his forehead. "Fuck, Regina..."

"That's your job." I rocked my hips up, encouraging him.

He responded, speeding up his thrusts. He pinned my wrists again; his body covered mine.

"Like it?" I whispered, feeling suddenly shy.

He turned his head and kissed me. "I want to live inside you."

I wrapped my arms around him. "I'll let you. Whoever orgasms first gets to be on top." My lips found the tender spot where his shoulder met neck. I kissed it, then bit down, clenching my lower muscles at the same time.

He lost it, thrashing above me. I waited until he stilled to slip my fingers into the wetness between us. A few strokes and my own orgasm flared and died.

Cole sagged onto me, gasping. "Regina, what the hell?"

"I cheated." I gave him a wink.

"Naughty girl."

"Always." I wriggled under him. "You should make me pay."

"Oh, I will," he promised. He rose up over me and I caught sight of his rock hard cock. "Cole," I said, wide-eyed. "Already?"

"I've waited a long time for this." He lay on his back, snapped his fingers and pointed to his upright cock. "Get riding. It's gonna be a long night."

10

"What I don't understand, is why you never made a move on me before now." We'd spent the last few hours working out our lust. After the last round, I'd taken a little nap and woken up in Cole's arms.

"Well for starters, the first time I saw you, you were six and I was twelve."

I sat up enough to hit him with a pillow. "I know that. I mean when we were older."

"When we were older...I turned eighteen and you were still too young."

"But I looked older."

"Yes, you did. And you had trouble written all over you. Still do." He leaned in for a quick kiss. "So what about when I turned eighteen?"

"You were off to school. I wanted you to get out of this town as much as you did."

"You did?"

"I knew you didn't like it. I hoped...I hoped you'd stay away."

I touched his arm, tracing the lean muscle there. "Why?"

"Because I didn't trust myself around you. Because I thought you deserved better than me. And as much as I wanted you, I wanted you to have a good life. I figured you'd find better opportunity outside of this town."

"And when I returned early? When I was twenty?"

"I'd just started my sheriff campaign. I went all in, even though I didn't expect to win the first time around. I just didn't have time to give." He pulled me close, with a hand on my hip. "Should've stalked you and handcuffed you to the bed the minute you turned eighteen."

"Better late than never." I melted into him, feeling the ties of our past, and our future, binding us together.

"So what now?" I asked. My cheek pressed to Cole's chest. "Am I still your naughty maid?"

"Only on weekdays. On my days off, I may just keep you chained to my bed."

"Ooh, a real love slave."

"I mean it. I'm not letting you go."

I sat up and put a finger to his lips, feeling them curve into a smile. "I know."

We made out for a while, and then Cole went to clean up. When he returned, the sight of him, shirtless with boxers hanging low on his lean hips, nearly set me off again.

I bounced out of bed. "Let's celebrate."

"How?"

"Post-coital ice cream."

"I don't eat junk food."

I rolled my eyes. "Of course you don't."

Ten minutes later, we were at the Licking Hole corner store. I felt a little nervous when Cole came to open the truck door. It was the first time I'd be seen in public with the sheriff, who was a minor celebrity around these parts. And it was close to eleven pm on a Thursday night. The corner store was a popular hangout spot; we were certain to run into someone we knew.

Cole took my hand and I forgot all that, until we hit the freezer aisle. A skinny blonde, wearing a frown, brightened when she saw Cole.

"Sheriff?"

Lucy Litt, my old nemesis. She was trim and cute even in yoga pants. Or especially in yoga pants.

"Miss Litt," Cole drawled like the good ole boy he was. "Good evening."

"I haven't seen you since the Policeman's ball," she gushed. Her eyes flicked up and down every inch of Cole's six feet, lingering at the halfway point. "I guess you're too busy to catch up with an old friend." Her pout made me want to vomit.

"Not at all, Miss Litt. You remember Regina? I think you were in school together."

Lucy's smile turned plastic. "Regina? What a nice surprise," she said, and meant the total opposite.

"Yes, it is nice." I wore a fake smile of my own.

"What are you two doing here?"

"Just getting ice cream," I said, opening a freezer and grabbing a pint. "Not staying long."

"I had a question, actually, about some of the crime going on in town," Lucy said. "I hear it's mainly based in the trailer park—Regina, you know the one."

I gritted my teeth as Lucy shot Cole a brilliant smile.

"Sheriff Townsend, do you have a minute?"

"Of course. You go on, Regina." Cole held out some cash to me, and color flared into my cheeks. "I got it," I waved the bill away and stomped to the register.

They were still talking when I finished paying, their

blond heads close together. Cole illustrated a point with a graceful gesture. Lucy nodded, but when Cole turned away, she shot me a look of pure disgust.

I followed Cole out the door, but Lucy's expression stuck in my mind. With a few words, she sent me back to grade school, where I was the scruffy, ugly outcast. I was the girl from the wrong neighborhood and everyone knew it. Between the kids and teachers, they made sure I did too.

I remembered why I was so desperate to leave. You can't change who you are in Licking Hole. People decided who you were, and you were stuck for life.

Cole stopped at a stoplight on Main Street, and I sank down in the seat. I didn't want people to see us together.

It hit me. I was the special one. The one he'd waited for. But I couldn't have him. People would talk—it would hurt him, really hurt him. He'd worked so hard on his image. And his image was his career. Just being with me risked his career.

By the time we got home, I'd made my decision. The community needed him more than I did.

"You're quiet," he said as he held the door for me. "You must be really hungry."

I walked through the kitchen straight to the hall to the bedroom.

"Regina?" He followed me, frowning as I started packing my clothes. "What are you doing?"

"I can't do this, Cole," I said, swallowing the lump in my throat. "You need to take me back to the trailer."

His hands caught mine. "Look at me."

"No." I ducked my head.

"Look at me," he repeated, less gently, and caught my chin. "That's an order. You promised to obey me."

"I can't!" I wrenched myself away. "This isn't going to work."

"Why not?"

"I see how people look at me, and how they look at you. They'll think less of you, because you're with me. And if it ever gets out what you've done, the deal you gave me—"

"It's none of their business."

"It doesn't matter. It makes no sense that you'd be with me."

"I made a vow."

"Yes, to the community. And they're expecting—"

"No. Before that. I vowed I would take care of you."

"What?"

"You were twelve years old."

"I knew what I wanted. I knew who I wanted." He ran a hand over his buzzed head. "I'm nothing if not committed. You said that yourself. When I was eighteen, I told myself I'd wait for you. Don't you see, Regina? You're the only one for me."

"It can't be, Cole. People won't respect you. I'm like a stain on your shining armor. Did you see Lucy Litt's face when she realized I was with you?"

"I don't care about what people like her think."

"You should. Those people elect you."

"Listen to me. You're not thinking clearly. You never have."

"I'm not drunk—"

"I mean about yourself. You don't see yourself like I see you. Like anyone sees you." You're special. You're sweet and passionate, and funny. And you go out of your way to help people. You're a good person."

"Tell that to Mr. Roberts."

"I don't have to. He told me. He knew you were in trouble, and wouldn't accept help from anybody. He came to me because he knew I was the only one who could make you accept help. He cares about you."

I shook my head. "I don't?"

"You dropped out of college to help your mom. You spent one day at the Orchard, and the residents all love you."

"They don't count. Next time I see them they won't know who I am."

"Then you'll charm them all over again." He wrapped his arms around me.

"I can't do it. I can't spend the rest of my life fighting against my reputation in this town."

"Then don't. Forget what people think. Except me. Listen to me now, when I tell you how special you are." He dropped his head and rested it on my forehead. "I'll spend the rest of my life convincing you."

"You deserve someone better."

"I waited for you. For years, I waited to be with you. There is no one else for me."

God, he broke my heart. But this was for the best. He was a good sheriff. I couldn't let him throw away his life on me.

"I'm sorry, Cole." I stepped away and picked up my bag, holding it between us like a shield. "This was fun but it couldn't last. When you get married to someone like Lucy Litt, tell her you just were slumming it with me."

"Regina." His voice almost stopped me in my tracks. Almost.

I got halfway down the hall. Cole reached around me and grabbed the bag, pulling it easily out of my hands. He threw it aside before reaching for me.

"Cole, what the hell—"

His shoulder hit my middle, and he tossed me up like I

weighed nothing. Pivoting, he carried me back to the bedroom, kicking the door shut. He flopped me down on the bed and grabbed my hand.

"What the fuck are you doing—no!"

I struggled as I heard the clink of metal cuffs. Goddam Cole handcuffed me to the bed. He sat back and grinned at me, and all I could do was glare.

"You can't keep me here forever."

"Yes, I can." The gleam in his eyes told me not only would he do it, he'd love every second of it.

Despite myself, I got wet.

"Dammit, Cole!" I struggled to no avail.

"Careful. Don't hurt yourself."

"The minute I break free I am throwing these cuffs in the garbage."

Cole straddled me, and unbuttoned my jeans. "I work as a cop. I have access to a thousand more."

"Goddammit!" I thrashed, but his weight held me down. "I'm gonna burn your house down."

"You might want to keep a civil tongue in your head if you ever want me to let you go."

I quieted. He was right. "Cole, please let me go."

Scooting down on the bed, he peeled off my jeans. Catching my ankle, he kissed it, tickling it with his stubble. "No."

"Goddammit!" I kicked out again, and he held down my legs, lay down, put his mouth against the gusset of my panties and—

"Oooooh."

He worked his tongue over me, probing through the silken fabric. The handcuffs rattled against the headboard for a different reason.

After a few minutes, I stiffened. "Cole, I—"

"Come for me, sweetheart."

My back arched, my whole body tightened, and I shouted my orgasm to the ceiling.

"That's one," he said, kissing my midriff. "A few more of those and I bet you'll stay."

"Maybe." I stared at the ceiling so the room would stop spinning. Why had I been about to leave?

"I'll keep you naked and chained up, and take you out once a year to show you off at the Policeman's Ball. But only after I've fucked you into submission."

An image of Lucy Litt floated through my head. "Where everyone will wonder why when you're going to settle down with a suitable woman and 'take out the trash.'"

Cole lifted his head. "They wouldn't dare."

"Believe me, I've heard worse. And not just from the likes of Lucy Litt."

"You really care about what people like her think?"

"Well, yeah. Don't you?"

"No. And anyway, you're smarter than her and most of the town put together."

"That's not hard. Her brains are all in her yoga pants."

Cole snorted. "I didn't notice."

I rolled my eyes.

"So you want to leave because of what people will think. Do you care about what I think?"

"No," I said, because I knew it was a trap.

"Regina..."

"Fine. Yes, Cole, I care about what you think."

"Good." He sat up and settled himself between my legs. "Because I'm going to tell you."

I closed my eyes.

"Regina look at me."

"No."

I squeezed my eyes shut.

"Regina."

I opened my eyes. *Please be gentle*, I pleaded with them.

"You were always...how do I say this?" he paused. "You were always..."

I held my breath.

"Amazing. You were a pretty little girl but you grew up so fast and you were gorgeous." His tone was reverent. "I used to notice you everywhere. And I tried not to stare—I knew how messed up that was. So I made my vow, and I waited. And the whole time I waited, I hoped you would leave, and get out of town. There was nothing for you here. Nothing but me."

"That's all the reason I need. But Cole, I don't deserve you."

"Please. I'm the one who doesn't deserve you."

"Tell me how that is possible."

He shrugged. "I'll never go very far."

"You're sheriff! You won an election when you were twenty-eight!"

"Only because my opponent, the incumbent, died the night before of a heart attack. And I still only took sixty-two percent."

I rolled my eyes. "Still, Cole. You were born to be sheriff and make everyone follow the rules."

"Yeah, and how much further can I go in my career? I'm twenty-eight and I've reached my peak."

"Please," I huffed. "You could be mayor."

"Mayor of Licking Hole."

We stared at each other for a moment and then burst out laughing.

"I could just see you making jokes in your head." His shoulders shook with mirth.

"Oh my god, Cole." My abs hurt so bad from laughing I almost cried. "We have to move."

"Maybe one day," he said. "If that's what you really want."

I stopped laughing. "Really? You'd leave—for me?"

He nodded. "If you decide that's what you really want." His elegant hands cupped my face.

"Stay with me," he said. "Hide my cuffs, burn my house down. Drive me fucking crazy. Just don't leave me."

All of a sudden, the Lucy Litts of the world didn't matter so much. What could compare to this beautiful man between my legs?

"I don't know," I said. He looked so hurt I decided I couldn't tease him anymore. "Are you going to tie me up and abuse me every night?"

"Every night." He kissed me.

"Okay. I'll do it." I smiled against his lips. "And Cole?"

"Yes?"

"You can lick my hole. Anytime."

He groaned. "That's it." He rolled out of bed. "I'm getting the gag."

"You love it!" I shouted after him. Smiling, I leaned back, wriggling back into the headboard to give my arms more slack. I might as well get comfortable cuffed to the sheriff's of Licking Hole's headboard, because there was no place I'd rather be.

FREE BOOK

Get your FREE copy of Beauty & The Lumberjacks: https://BookHip.com/WZLTMQX

After this logging season, I'm never having sex again. Because: *reasons.*

But first, I have a gig earning room and board and ten thousand dollars by 'entertaining' eight lumberjacks.

Eight strong and strapping Paul Bunyan types, big enough to break me in two.

There's Lincoln, the leader, the stern, silent type...

Jagger, the Kurt Cobain look-alike, with a soul full of music and rockstar moves...

Elon & Oren, ginger twins who share everything...

Saint, the quiet genius with a monster in his pants...

Roy and Tommy, who just want to watch...

And Mason, who hates me and won't say why, but on his night tries to break me with pleasure...

They own me: body, mind and orgasms.

But when they discover my secret—the reason I'm hiding from the world—everything changes.

Click here to read Beauty and the Lumberjacks for free

ALSO BY LEE SAVINO

For film and TV rights inquiries: <u>lee.savino@</u>
<u>leesavino.com</u>

Contemporary Romance

Royally Bad
Royally Fake Fiancé

Her Marine Daddy
Her Dueling Daddies
Beauty & The Lumberjacks
Snowed in with the Lumberjack
Rescuing Regina

Dark Mafia Romance

Mafia Brides
Revenge is Sweet
Vengeance is Mine

A Dark Mafia Romance trilogy with Stasia Black
Innocence
Awakening
Queen of the Underworld

Beauty and the Rose trilogy with Stasia Black
Beauty's Beast
Beauty & the Thorns
Beauty & the Rose

Paranormal romance

Berserker Saga
Sold to the Berserkers
Mated to the Berserkers
Bred by the Berserkers (FREE novella only available at
www.leesavino.com)
Taken by the Berserkers
Given to the Berserkers
Claimed by the Berserkers
Rescued by the Berserker
Captured by the Berserkers
Kidnapped by the Berserkers
Bonded to the Berserkers
Berserker Babies
Night of the Berserkers
Owned by the Berserkers
Tamed by the Berserkers
Mastered by the Berserkers
Surrendered to the Berserkers

Berserker Warriors
Aegir
Siebold with Ines Johnson

Bad Boy Alphas with Renee Rose

Alpha's Temptation
Alpha's Danger
Alpha's Prize
Alpha's Challenge
Alpha's Obsession
Alpha's Desire
Alpha's War
Alpha's Mission
Alpha's Bane
Alpha's Secret
Alpha's Prey
Alpha's Sun

Shifter Ops with Renee Rose
Alpha's Moon
Alpha's Vow
Alpha's Revenge
Alpha's Fire
Alpha's Rescue
Alpha's Command

Midnight Doms with Renee Rose
Alpha's Blood
His Captive Mortal
The Virgin and the Vampire
(All Souls' Night anthology exclusive)

Werewolves of Wallstreet with Renee Rose
Big Bad Boss: Midnight

Sci fi romance

Planet of Kings with Tabitha Black
Brutal Mate
Brutal Claim
Brutal Capture
Brutal Beast
Brutal Demon

Tsenturion Warriors with Golden Angel
Alien Captive
Alien Tribute
Alien Abduction

Dragons in Exile with Lili Zander
Draekon Mate
Draekon Fire
Draekon Heart
Draekon Abduction
Draekon Destiny
Daughter of Draekons
Draekon Fever
Draekon Rogue
Draekon Holiday

Draekon Rebel Force with Lili Zander
Draekon Warrior
Draekon Conqueror
Draekon Pirate
Draekon Warlord
Draekon Guardian

Cowboy Romance

Rocky Mountain Mail Order Brides
Rocky Mountain Dawn
Rocky Mountain Bride
Rocky Mountain Rose
Rocky Mountain Romp
Rocky Mountain Rogue
Rocky Mountain Daddy
Rocky Mountain Ride
Possessing Pearl

Cowboy Brides - A domestic discipline anthology

Wild Whip Ranch with Tristan River
Cowboy's Babygirl
Taming His Wild Girl

ABOUT THE AUTHOR

USA today bestselling author Lee Savino has written over 69 steamy romance novels. Bad boys, mafia men, wolf shifters, and dragon shifters in space—her dominant, alpha-hole heroes will stop at nothing to possess their one true love. Happily-ever-after and book hangover guaranteed!

Download a free book at leesavino.com.

Connect with Lee Savino in her fabulous Goddess Group:
https://www.facebook.com/groups/LeeSavino